Just One Spark

The Kingston Family
Book 4

NEW YORK TIMES BESTSELLING AUTHOR
Carly Phillips

JUST ONE SPARK

I was living the rock-and-roll dream—loud nights, fast women, and zero regrets. Until a baby scare nearly blows up my life.

Lesson learned. I need to change my hard-partying ways. My PR team insists a fake girlfriend will clean up my playboy image.

I say only one woman will do. Cassidy Forrester. Gorgeous. Grounded. And the woman I left alone in a hotel room after one mind-blowing night together.

For the sake of the band, she agrees to play the part. But when it comes to Cassidy, I'm not pretending.

My feelings for her sent me running once, but now I'm all in, and I intend to prove we are meant to be.

CHAPTER ONE

Dash

A COUPLE OF months ago, I was living the dream. I had women at my beck and call. More money than I'd ever dreamed of earning doing something I love. Bandmates who are my best friends, and success beyond my wildest dreams. I still have those things, but I also have a huge weight sitting on my chest in the form of an outstanding paternity test, courtesy of one night with a woman I barely remember and whose name I hadn't known at the time.

Word has spread over social media, television entertainment and celebrity news, and whatever magazines still show up in grocery store checkout lines. Instead of talk about the band's music and our new drummer, Axel Forrester, there is speculation about whether the Original Kings' lead singer has impregnated a one-night stand.

Talk about a wake-up call.

I glance around my patio, where clusters of people are gathered talking. The professionals stand on one side, the roadies and groupies, the women who want to fuck a rock star, laugh and party on the other. My band members are scattered around, all having fun on a hot late-September day in East Hampton, with the alcohol at my expense.

Whose idea was a party when my entire world might be falling apart? I run a hand through my hair and decided to head over to my brother Xander's house, about a mile down the road. Though I could walk, I decide to take my baby, a Ferrari Limited-Edition V12 supercar. Not even the power of the engine or the yellow racing stripe I love help my mood.

On the short ride, I think about the many mistakes I've made in life and decide I can do better. And though I know, if the kid is mine, I'll step up, I pray to God I'll dodge this bullet. Panic-induced sweat breaks out on my skin, and I pump up the air conditioner.

When I arrive at Xander's, my other brother Linc's car is sitting in the driveway. So I'll have both brothers to hang out with. I let myself inside and hear their voices coming from the kitchen.

I walk into the huge room where Linc and Xander are sitting at the table. "Hey."

They look up when I enter. "How are you holding up?" Linc asks.

I head to the refrigerator, open the door, and take out a can of Diet Coke. "Feeling like shit." I pop the top and guzzle a long sip.

"How long until you have news?" Xander asks.

"My lawyer should call me any minute. Hour. Day. Fuck!" I raise a hand and catch myself, not wanting to hit anything in my brother's kitchen. Or break my hand on the granite countertop.

Xander and Linc exchange knowing looks.

"Come on. Sit." Xander strides over, hooks an arm around my neck, and pulls him toward the chairs by the table. Releasing me, which I appreciate because I was choking, Xander then braces both palms on my shoulders and pushes until I drop into the chair.

"Look, I'd be as crazy as you are if it was happening to me, but right now the best thing you can do is calm the fuck down," Xander says.

"I know." And I do, but is it possible? Hell no.

Linc shakes his head. "I hope this goes without saying, but once you survive this scare, things need to change."

I do my best not to scowl or punch my brother for thinking now is a good time for life lectures.

"Linc, chill, yeah?" Xander gives Linc a pointed look.

"I'm just looking out for him," Linc says, leaning back in his chair, always the composed brother.

"I know you are." I get where Linc is coming from. I also noticed that Linc said *when* I survived this scare. Not if. Which means my oldest sibling has faith I might get through this unscathed. Not be a father. I just hope Linc is right.

Since our dead father hadn't been a good parent, Linc has always felt the need to herd the rest of the siblings and make sure we're taken care of. Whether we need his guidance or not. I don't blame him. Hell, I appreciate my oldest brother. I'm just not in the mood for a lecture.

I'm damned lucky the woman in question was willing to do a noninvasive DNA test. A blood sample from Mom, one from Dad, and a fetal cell analysis will provide a result that is ninety-nine percent accurate. The fact that the chick is willing to do one tells me she isn't a money-hungry gold-digger.

If I've knocked her up, I won't marry her, but she and the baby won't want for a damned thing, and I'll get to know my kid. My stomach cramps at the notion of having a baby with a stranger.

"Are the guys at your place?" Xander asks.

The question shakes me from my disturbing thoughts. "They were out by the pool when I left."

Xander folds his arms across his chest. "Any chance I'll have a houseful of people soon?" he asks, not sounding happy about it.

"You never know." I can't stop the grin lifting the corners of my mouth at Xander's predictable reaction.

I have made it my life's mission to drive my more solitary brother crazy by showing up uninvited all the time. Xander is uptight and can always use a good shaking up. But despite it all, we're close.

Now that Xander lives with his fiancée, I've stopped using my key and ring the bell instead. Unless I know I won't be interrupting them. Linc's car in the driveaway indicated it was safe to enter today. I have no desire to walk in on Xander and Sasha doing shit I don't need to see.

"Dash! I didn't know you were here, too." Sasha flows into the kitchen because that's what my brother's fiancée does. She glides across a room like the actress she is. Good thing she's down-to-earth, too.

"Hello, beautiful." I wink at her and catch Xander's glare.

I have every reason to suck up to Sasha. I recently crossed a line with Cassidy Forrester, Sasha's best friend and former personal assistant, despite both Xander and Sasha warning me against making a move. Things between us had escalated out of control after Sasha had been hurt by her stalker. Cassidy needed a shoulder to cry on, and I was admittedly struck dumb from the first time I laid eyes on her.

I acted with my dick and all my other body parts that were drawn to the California girl. Our one night had blown my mind, and even for a guy who's had more than his share of women, that is a huge under-statement.

I'd woken up as sober as when I slid into her the night before. No drunk excuses. Sunlight was stream-ing into the hotel room, illuminating her silky blond hair, porcelain skin, and delicate profile that would inspire songs in my future, and I'd freaked the fuck out. Instead of acting like a man, I got dressed and disappeared before she woke up. Things have been awkward since.

"Knock, knock, we're coming in!" I recognize my lead guitarist Jagger's voice followed by footsteps, letting me know Mac, the bassist, and Axel, the new drummer, who happens to be Cassidy's brother, are with him. And fuck no, Axel does not know what happened between me and his sister.

"In the kitchen," I call out.

"Really?" Xander asks, eyebrow raised in annoy-ance.

Sasha squeezes his shoulder. "It's fine."

"It's not. What's wrong with your house?" he asks me. "I love you but half the time it feels like you guys live here."

I lift my shoulders. "Our road manager came by, called a few friends…"

"There's a party at his place," Mac says as the guys filed into the kitchen dressed in bathing trunks and sneakers.

Sasha narrows her gaze. "Where's Cass?"

Cassidy used to be Sasha's personal assistant until the band's latest one quit. Xander, Sasha, and Harrison Dare, a movie star friend of hers, are creating a production company and have asked Cassidy to be their creative director. With her ad agency background prior to working for Sasha, she's a perfect fit.

But there's time before they'll need Cassidy to start work, so Axel convinced her to lend the band a hand in the meantime. Again, because Axel has no idea that I fucked his sister and walked out, making certain she understood what *one and done* meant. Because yeah, when I catch feelings, I'm that much of an asshole.

"She's at the pool, keeping an eye on shit," Axel says, wincing under Sasha's pissed-off glare.

Normally I would get the brunt of her anger, but Axel had been the last guy to leave the house. And he's Cassidy's brother.

"You left her there with your goddamn entourage and the groupies?" Sasha walks over and smacks me upside the head.

"Hey! I didn't do it," I grumble.

She shoots me a look that lets me know I've done other things to earn that swat, and I can't deny I deserve it. Nor can I fight with her in front of the band.

"Overseeing your parties and babysitting your

groupies isn't part of her job description." Sasha swipes a set of car keys that sits in a bowl on the counter.

"Where are you going?" Xander asks.

"To save my best friend." She waves at Xander with a warm smile that I have to admit would make any man envious, ignores the rest of us, and strides out of the kitchen.

"Good job," Xander mutters. "Way to piss her off."

I run a hand over my face. "Look, I have a lot on my mind!"

Xander looks at me, his jaw tight, and I don't say a word. Of my two brothers, I can read Xander better. And Xander wants to give me the same lecture Linc did.

When this nightmare is over, I need to get my shit together. ASAP.

★ ★ ★

Cassidy

I SIT ON the edge of the saltwater gunite pool and dip my feet into the warm water, ignoring the half-naked groupies hanging on to men who are friends with Dash Kingston, the owner of this East Hampton home.

"I want a raise," I say out loud to no one in particular. Because I sure as hell don't get paid enough to babysit the entourage of the Original Kings, an award-winning rock band, comprised of man-child idiots who do what they want, when they want, everyone else be damned.

My actual title is personal assistant to the band, a job I only took as a favor to my brother. The four core members have disappeared, leaving me to deal with the people, party, and mess they'll leave behind. Nobody else will watch over the house and make sure these *guests* respect boundaries and stay outside.

Not that Dash deserves anything from me, but my brother does.

"Hey, Cass," a familiar female voice says.

I glance up, shading my eyes from the sun, just as my best friend, Sasha Keaton, joins me, sitting by my side and also dipping her bare feet into the pool.

"What are you doing here? Shouldn't you be home with your hot fiancé?"

Sasha leans back, her hands behind her on the bluestone patio. "When the guys showed up, I figured you'd want company."

I smile. "And that's why I love you."

"Back at you," Sasha says, tilting her face toward the sun.

Sasha and I had been based in Los Angeles, traveling to locations where Sasha filmed until a couple of months ago, when she came to New York for a role. I, as her then-personal assistant, joined her. Sasha and Xander Kingston, Dash's brother and the author of the book on which the movie was based, had history they then rekindled. After filming ended, Sasha had decided to move across the country to be with Xander and, along with him, open a production company with another famous actor, Harrison Dare.

I eventually plan to work for their new company, K-Talent Productions, a name they've recently updated, but for now I've agreed to help the band until they can hire someone they agree on permanently.

"I came to take you to Xander's. You don't need to babysit the house," Sasha says.

"I take it the band made their way over there?" I ask.

Sasha nods. "If they don't want to be here, there's no reason for you to be, either. Let's go hang out at my place."

I grin.

"What?"

"I like that you consider Xander's house *your place*. I'm glad you're happy." My friend had soared to stardom, sacrificing her relationship with Xander in the process. But in the end, things have worked out and they both deserve it.

"I want the same thing for you. So while we're alone, I just wanted to make sure you're not upset with me," Sasha says. She lifts her feet out of the pool, and we both stand and reach for towels on the chairs behind us.

"Why would I be?" I ask while drying my legs.

Sasha does the same before sitting down to buckle her sandals as she replies. "I know you don't want to be around Dash, but when Xander and Axel asked if the band could borrow your talents for a short time, I couldn't lie. It's going to take a while to get the paperwork for the new business going, and Harrison is finishing up a movie. We all have downtime now."

"I know. And I didn't have to say yes when Axel asked. This job isn't your doing. It's my brother's and that's because he has no idea I slept with Dash." I wince at the reminder of the best night of my life that had ended in the most humiliating morning after.

"I want to throttle Dash for being such an asshole," Sasha mutters.

There's nothing I can say to that since I agree. And if Axel finds out, he'll kill Dash himself.

Our parents died in a car accident when I was five and Axel was seven. Our grandmother then raised us until she passed away, leaving an eighteen-year-old Axel to deal with me, a sixteen-year-old girl just finding herself. Though I feel like we'd looked out for each other, Axel has deemed himself my father figure and still acts as such.

Sasha sighs. "Yeah. I've seen how overprotective Axel can be. I don't think he'd take the news well, and the last thing you want is an issue between the band's lead singer and their new member. They have enough crazy publicity as it is," she says.

"Agreed." Neither one of us mentions Dash's baby scare out loud.

Sasha probably doesn't want to hurt me by discussing it. And I don't want to puke into the man's million-dollar pool. I'm aware based on the timing that he slept with the woman before he'd been with me. Not that it matters. He hadn't been *with* me in any way that inspires loyalty or monogamy. But the thought of Dash fathering some rando's baby makes me want to alternatively be sick and cry. How could I have let myself fall for the proverbial rock star?

A shriek comes from the far side of the grass. Both Sasha and I turn to see one of the big-breasted women pull off her bikini top and jump into the deep end of the pool. Three men shuck their shorts and follow.

"Oh. My. God." I spin away, not needing to see more.

"Come on. Let's get out of here." Sasha gathers her things, and I pull my cover-up over my bathing suit and slip into her flip-flops, happy to join my friend and leave this hedonistic nightmare behind.

Dash

I'M HUDDLED IN the corner of the overly large sofa in Xander's family room. While grumbling about too many people in his house, Xander has moved the band and Linc to a space with more sitting room. Status quo for my best-selling thriller author brother, whose books are made into hit movies. He likes a more solitary life.

Why Xander puts up with me and my shit is beyond me. But I love my older brother and always have. I pulled the same crap when we were kids, sleeping on the floor of Xander's bedroom until our mother bought a trundle bed so I was more comfortable.

Xander had grumbled then, too, I think wryly. But if my life goes to hell, Xander will be there and not say, *I told you so*. Not much, anyway.

My cell rings, silencing everyone. I pull out the phone from my pocket, glance at the screen, and my heart begins to pound harder in my chest.

"It's the lawyer," I say to my audience, men I trust with his life. Men who've been waiting to hear the news along with me. The band, because of the publicity I've thrust on them, but like my brothers, they also care.

Palms slick with sweat, I stand. I take the call, putting it on speaker because I don't want to have to repeat the news if it's bad. "Peter, talk to me," I say to my attorney.

"Got the paternity results in my hand," the man says.

At that moment, Sasha walks in, Cassidy by her side. Because why shouldn't the woman who affects me on a soul-deep level witness my humiliation?

"Dash, you are *not* the father," Peter says without wasting time, and damned if I don't drop to my knees in relief and disconnect the call.

"Fucking sounds like an episode of *Maury*," Axel says. "But you must be relieved. Congrats, man."

Linc and Xander surround me, and I rise to my feet, promising myself that, from this point on, my life will change. No more fucking groupies, no more being too wasted as an excuse.

I blink, my gaze refocusing until I meet Cassidy's damp stare, her pretty green eyes wet with unshed tears. She's wrapped her arms around herself and my stomach cramps at the hurt I see in her expression. Unable to deal with the pain I caused when I was still in the process of reconfiguring what I want out of life, I turn away.

"I think everyone should go back to your place and send the partiers home." Xander squeezes my shoulder. "You stay here and calm down. You can head back when you know it's quiet there."

I incline my head. "Sounds like a good idea." I turn to the band. "Guys? I appreciate the support but I need some time."

One by one they slap me on the shoulder and head out the door, each giving me a word of congratulations as they leave.

And when I turn back to face Sasha and Cassidy, the women are nowhere to be found.

★　★　★

Cassidy

NEEDING SPACE, I walk into the kitchen of Xander and Sasha's home. I head straight to the counter, brace my hands on the granite, and dip my head, releasing a long-held sigh. Dash is not the father of some groupie's baby.

Why the hell am I so relieved? After the way he'd treated me, why do I care?

A little over two months ago, I met Dash Kingston, and the floor beneath me had shaken as if an earthquake hit, and having been born and bred in LA,

I've experienced plenty of them. My reaction had been ridiculous. As an assistant to an A-list actress, I've met more handsome men than I can count. I had recently been dumped by a man I thought I loved. Yet, standing in a club full of people, I'd taken one look at the lead singer of the Original Kings, and it was like no one else was in the room. And damned if he hadn't stared back at me, looking shaken, as if he felt the same way.

Later that night, when I'd been mistaken for Sasha and attacked by my friend's stalker, Dash was frantic. He'd even gone to the hospital and waited there to make sure I was okay. Not the actions of an unaffected man. Which is why, after Sasha had been attacked and I panicked, I'd given in to the attraction and need.

I thought I was different than his other women. The groupies. Until I woke up alone the morning after, and he'd never mentioned our night together again. I close my eyes, trying to rid myself of the painful memory, only to recall the panic on his face when he'd been on the phone with his lawyer just now. And the sheer relief when he heard the paternity results and realized his entire life wouldn't be upended.

I was happy for him. Stupid, stupid, stupid.

"Are you finished with the self-flagellation?" Sasha asks. She'd followed me out of the room filled with men congratulating Dash and, as a good friend, gave me a few minutes to pull myself together.

I stand up and straighten my shoulders, only to find Sasha staring, her gaze narrowed.

"What?" I ask.

"It's not terrible to still have feelings," Sasha says, quietly so nobody can overhear.

I shrug. "I don't have feelings unless you count being happy for him that he dodged a bullet." We both knew I'm lying. "That's what I don't understand about myself. Why do I care after he was such an ass?"

"Because you're a good person, Cass. Are you sure you want to work with them?" Sasha asks.

I nod. "This week is a radio interview. The first with the entire band since Axel joined them. The focus will turn to music, the guys will hunker down in the studio, and all will be fine." At least that's the story I'm telling myself.

"Okay then." Sasha glances at her watch. "I need to take a call, but I'll drive you back to Dash's house right after. I shouldn't be long."

"I'll take her. I'm going home, anyway."

I jerk, surprised by the sound of Dash's voice. He stands in the entry to the kitchen. He wears a pair of swim trunks and an open button-down shirt, and his tanned, lickable abs are on display. His jet-black hair has been recently cut and it's longer on top, looking like he's been running his fingers through it in agitation.

Of all the Kingston brothers, I think Dash is the best-looking, his face lean, his features chiseled. He has full lips and he knows how to use them to give maximum pleasure. At the reminder, I fold my arms across my chest, covering my nipples so he can't see how he affects me.

Sasha glances at Dash. "I don't think that's a good idea."

"Actually, it's a perfect idea," I say. "Dash and I can discuss what he and the band need from me." I shoot Sasha a reassuring gaze. Though I appreciate the support, I can handle Dash.

"Okay." Although Sasha's forehead wrinkles in worry, she walks over and gives me a hug, which I gratefully return. Sasha is the sister I've never had, and I love her.

Sasha strides out of the kitchen, pausing to whisper something in Dash's ear that causes him to wince. A threat to the family jewels if he hurts me again, no doubt.

"Are you ready?" he asks.

I nod. I left my handbag in the kitchen, so I grab it from the chair it's sitting on, and follow him out, coming to a stop in front of the almost-five-hundred-thousand-dollar sports car. This I know from my brother and his obsession with them.

"Boys and their toys," I mutter as he opens the

door for me.

Dash chuckles, the sound a low rasp in my ear I'm eager to escape, but as I slide into the low-slung seat, I catch a whiff of his familiar, musky scent. I inhale, and arousal hits low in my abdomen as he shuts the door, leaving me in the small interior, surrounded by the heady cologne. Already, I regret not waiting for Sasha to drive me back.

There is no conversation thanks to the loud engine revving as he drives, but when he pulls into his long driveway, he parks the car and cuts the motor.

Before I can find the door handle and escape, he speaks. "Cassidy, wait."

My hand freezes and I have no choice but to turn toward him.

He places his tanned, inked forearm onto the top of my seat, bringing us together in the small car. I've already been inhaling his scent and getting worked up enough to squirm in my seat. Now his handsome face is too close for comfort. I've gone from thinking we should clear things up between us to wanting to get away from his magnetic pull.

"What do you want?" I ask.

"You said we should talk about what the band needs from you," Dash says.

I roll my eyes. "I know how to do my job. I just didn't want to make Sasha go out of her way to take me to my car when you were leaving anyway." I pivot toward the door, intending to make my getaway.

"I'm sorry." His low tone reminds me of the rumbling voice on stage that has women throwing their panties at his feet.

But damn him, his words stop me from leaving. "You're sorry. For what?"

If he's going to apologize, I want him to spell out what he's done wrong.

"Look at me and I'll tell you," he says.

I turn. The man across from me isn't the cocky rock star who struts around on stage like he owns the world. This Dash Kingston appears to be a mere mortal, not a rock god. He is a man who's been humbled by his actions. Although I don't kid myself that he'd be apologizing otherwise, I can't help but respond to the real person behind the cocky façade he presents to everyone else.

I raise my eyebrows, waiting for him to explain.

A muscle pulls in his jaw. "I shouldn't have left you the morning after without saying goodbye. That was a shitty thing to do."

"Yeah, it was." I blow out a breath, relieved he didn't apologize for sleeping with me. I don't think I could deal with being one of his regrets.

"I should have dealt with things better." He runs a hand through his already disheveled hair. "Hell, Cass. I should have handled *you* better."

Glad he not only recognizes he'd treated me like one of his groupies and pleased he's acknowledged it out loud, I decide to put my night with Dash where it belongs. "Thanks, Dash. It's in the past but I appreciate the apology."

Forcing a smile I don't feel, at least not in my heart, where somehow this man has gotten to me, I turn and let myself out of the car.

CHAPTER TWO

Dash

THE NIGHT AFTER finding out the paternity results, I sleep like the dead for the first time since the nightmare began. With that weight off my chest, I'm able to look to the future. The band. My lyrics. My family.

This morning, me and the guys are at a satellite radio station for an interview about our new member and the direction we plan to take our music. Along for the day is our publicist, Naomi Smith, and Cassidy, who has just returned from picking up a coffee order for us all.

Despite my apology, she still avoids me when she can, and I don't blame her. Our night together was staggering in its intensity, and I blew her off afterward, treating her like shit. It will take more than an apology to make it up to her. Now that my mind is clear of worry, I can focus again, and *she* is all I can see.

But right now I have an interview to focus on, and the host has started out brutal and isn't letting up. Lester Jones is a wannabe musician who never made it big, yet somehow became an influential critic and interviewer at *Rolling Stone* and *Vice* before gaining his own slot on satellite radio. He played with a band at the same music festivals as the Original Kings in our pre-fame days but never got the same audience support or response. He's resented us ever since.

As an interviewer, he's known for being a dick, so here we are. Me in a black tee and jeans, the pretentious asshole wearing a sport jacket and dress shirt, looking down his nose at me.

"Why did Dominic quit?" The prick seems focused on me, and not the other members of the band.

"You'll have to ask him." I refuse to discuss my friend's problems. I've been being grilled for the last ten minutes and I'm getting sick of it.

"Is it true he's addicted to blow?" the jackwad continues.

I stiffen. "Same answer. Move on or we're out of here," I mutter, adjusting the shades I wear because the sun is streaming in through the plate-glass window along the back wall.

A glance at Mac, Axel, and Jagger, shifting in their seats, drinking their caffeine, tells me they are just as wired as I am.

The next questions are aimed at Axel, and they're softballs in comparison, for which I'm grateful.

I remember Dominic tossing a drink in an interviewer's face when he hadn't liked the man's tone, and I don't know Axel well enough yet to gauge his temperament. At least he isn't on drugs like Dom had been.

"We all know Caged Chaos broke up so Denny could go solo," Lester is saying of Axel's former lead singer. "But why join the Original Kings?"

Axel drums his ringed fingers on the table in front of us. "Good music, solid guys, why the fuck not?"

I can't hold back my laugh because clearly Axel thinks this guy is as much of an asshole as I do.

Lester frowns and turns his gaze to me again. "It's all over the news that you aren't the father of Daisy Masterson's baby. How relieved are you?"

My eyebrows rise high, and I shoot an annoyed look at Naomi, who set up this gig. As part of the interview agreement, the subject of the paternity test has been deemed off-limits.

"Calm down," she mouths at me through the glass that separates the studio from the outer room.

I glance at Cassidy, who sits beside her, watching us, a frown on her lips. Though I'd fucked Daisy before I was with Cassidy, after the news broke and Daisy accused me publicly, facing the one woman whose opinion matters had been humiliating.

I manage to pull in a deep breath and reply to Lester through my clenched jaw. "I'm just glad the truth is out."

"Must have been a tense couple of weeks while you waited for the results."

I wonder if Lester wants to keep his teeth. As this is live, I hold my temper and curl my hands into tight fists beneath the table. "Next subject."

Lester places an elbow on the table and leans closer to the mic. "Your reputation as, shall we say, a ladies' man precedes you. Will this baby scare impact your future behavior?" The bastard's eyes dance with glee. He knows damned well he's violating our agreement but obviously thinks it'll be worth it.

Well, fuck him. I didn't sign up for this.

I slam my hands onto the table and push myself up until I tower over the other man. "Interview over. Hope you're happy."

I storm out of the room, ignoring Naomi, who'd let the questions go unchecked, and Cassidy, who I just don't want to face. The guys can wrap things up.

I shove open the glass doors that lead to the main reception area. Instead of taking the elevator, I jog down the stairs, relieved when I burst out of the building and into the humid New York City air. Add Dash Kingston to the list of top ten rock stars who've walked out on interviews. I don't give a shit. Not when I went there to discuss the band and our music, not my personal life.

I've had enough fucking coverage of my past to last a lifetime. While the baby daddy drama has dragged on, the online sites have exploited every dirty bit of drama they can find. As if a trashed room—thanks to drunk groupies and roadies who partied with the band—or women who claimed they'd fucked me after a concert are proof of fatherhood or some other culpability.

I look around for something to kick or punch and realize I'll only end up with a broken hand courtesy of a brick wall or splattering garbage across the sidewalk. I need an hour at the gym with a punching bag.

"Dash? Are you okay?"

I turn at the sound of Cassidy's voice. Concern I'm not sure I deserve etches her features.

She steps closer and I take her in, her blond hair in a high ponytail I want to wrap around my hand and yank while her red lips suck my dick. That would be one way to alleviate my current frustration. One that will not be happening any time soon.

Wishing I could adjust my cock, which stands at attention at the sight of her, I meet her gaze. "Yeah. Just not in the mood for that asshole to ask questions that won't do a damned thing to boost the band's presence or public awareness." Not in a positive manner, anyway.

"Naomi is going to ban them from future interviews," Cassidy murmurs.

"Too bad this one was live." I drag a hand through my hair and let out a groan. "I want to be taken seriously as an artist and not be fodder for gossip and bullshit."

"Then may I suggest you not give them a reason to focus more on your personal life than your music?" Naomi steps up beside us, the band along with her.

After scowling at her, I glance at the guys. "You finish the interview?"

All three shake their heads. "Fucker didn't play by the rules. We walked out, too," Axel says, surprising me because he's new to our group yet supporting me.

"We're a team," Jagger says.

"What he said." Mac shoves his hands into his pants pockets.

Naomi rolls her eyes. "Okay, nice love fest and you're all correct. Lester was an ass and he's on our company's shit list now. I don't care how influential he is. He has to follow the rules."

Our limousine pulls up to the curb. We'd driven from the Hamptons in the spacious vehicle that fit everyone, picking up Naomi at the satellite Midtown office of her LA PR firm on the way.

"Get in, guys, Cassidy. It's time for a talk." Naomi barks out orders like a drill sergeant.

The driver has exited the limo and walks around to

the sidewalk to open the back door. We all make our way inside, and the driver shuts the door, returns to his seat, and soon eases into traffic.

"He's going to drive around while we talk. Then you can all let him know where you want to go." Naomi sits back against the bench seat and crosses one leg over the other.

She's attractive in a take-no-prisoners way, which the band needs. Her dark brown bob is cut severely at her chin, and those equally brown eyes miss nothing that goes on around her.

"Let's start with the obvious," she begins. "You don't walk out on an interview." She clicks her long black polished nails against the car trim.

"That wasn't an interview, it was an ambush." I raise my voice, and to my shock, Cassidy, who's somehow ended up sitting beside me, puts a hand on my thigh to calm me.

As a distraction, it works. I relax my muscles and ease back against the seat, and she immediately removes her hand. I miss the warm sensation of her touch.

"I would have called things off except the interview was *live*. You don't want listeners thinking you can't handle yourself." Naomi's narrowed gaze holds mine until I blink first.

"Fine. I get it. But I had every right to walk out," I

say. "Nobody's going to treat me like shit just because his no-talent ass is holding a grudge."

Before anyone can ask, I give a brief explanation of my history with Lester Jones.

Naomi frowns. "Next time inform me of any potential issues before they surface. It would help me to do my job. On to the next point on my agenda. Dash mentioned wanting to change public focus from his personal life to that of the band and I agree," she says.

"It's what we all want," Axel says.

I'm glad to hear him speak up. I like my friends and especially my band members to speak their minds on any subject.

"So how do we manage that feat?" Jagger asks, tapping his foot on the carpeted floor.

"Lucky for you guys, I have a plan." A smile appears on Naomi's face that scares the crap out of me, and I don't frighten easily. "You," she says, pointing to me, "Need a steady, serious girlfriend."

"Are you fucking kidding me?" I feel like I'm about to eject out of my seat.

Jagger and Mac snicker, making their feelings on Naomi's idea known.

Axel appears amused, while Cassidy's eyes are wide, those pouty lips parted in shock.

"No," I say, in case anyone misinterpreted my earlier outburst.

"Not even with the right person?" Naomi asks, her calculating gaze sliding from me to the woman beside me.

"No way," Axel says, having caught Naomi glancing at Cassidy. He folds his arms across his chest. "Leave my sister out of this."

Cassidy blinks. "I'm not saying I want to do this, but it's my decision, Ax. Not yours." She speaks up for the first time, her tone determined.

"She's perfect," Naomi says, obviously sensing an opening to explain. "Cassidy is already a part of the band's inner circle, she's been around you guys for the last couple of weeks officially and for some time before that as Sasha's PA. That's more than enough time for a relationship to have developed while you were waiting for paternity news."

She draws a deep breath and continues, waving her hand through the air as she speaks. "Cassidy comforted you. Was there for you. And you just happened to fall in love. And bonus, she's practically a nun compared to those groupies who are always all over you."

"Gee, thanks," Cassidy mutters beside me.

"You're just getting over that asshole Adam. You don't need to get involved with anyone, let alone a musician."

Axel scowls because he knows what our lives are all about. But he has me wondering who this Adam guy is and what he means to her.

"Hey! How about not airing my personal life to your friends," Cassidy yells at her brother.

"Just think about it. Cassidy is a nice, wholesome girl. Exactly the type to settle the man-whore bachelor down. Sure, at first you'll both be news. Dash Kingston settles on one woman. A woman who looks, acts, and is different than any one-night muse who came before her." Naomi grins, obviously pleased with her idea. "Eventually you'll become boring. It will take you out of the news for your antics and get people to focus on what's important. The music."

Ignoring Naomi's unflattering description of me and sensing it's Cassidy who needs a subtle hug, this time I put a comforting hand on *her* thigh, ignoring the heat emanating from her skin beneath and the way I'm beginning to think my crazy publicist might just be on to something with this idea of hers.

★ ★ ★

Cassidy

WITH MY BROTHER growling in the seat across from me, Naomi gleefully happy, and Dash in shock, at least based on his silence, my stomach churns as the idea of being his fake girlfriend bounces around inside my head.

"All in favor?" Naomi asks.

"This isn't a group decision." Dash shoots his publicist a warning look. "It's between me and Cassidy, if we decide it's a smart way to go."

Mac and Jagger mutter their agreement, and though my brother glares, Axel remains silent.

It's obvious they defer to their lead singer, his potent power evident even offstage. Damn, it's hot. Sexy. And arousing thanks to the hand that remains on my thigh. I'm shocked my brother hasn't noticed.

Dash leans across the bench and Naomi and presses the driver's speaker button. "Stop the car at the next possible corner."

"Dash, what are you doing?" Naomi asks as the car comes to a halt.

He grasps my hand, and I stupidly curl her fingers around his. "We're going to discuss this alone. You know, the two people involved in your hairbrained idea?"

The driver opens the limo door, and Dash hops out, helping me as I awkwardly make my own way out of the vehicle.

"You don't have to do this, Cass."

I turn and meet my brother's worried gaze. "Don't worry about me. I'm a big girl and I can make my own decisions. It'll be fine." I hope.

Next thing I know, I'm standing on the corner of

Sixtieth Street and Third Avenue with Dash. The contrast of the air-conditioned limousine and the humid air smacks me in the face. God, I hate this weather and wish it would either turn cooler or the humidity would go away. At least my hair is pulled back so it isn't wild around my face.

"Dash, what is your plan?"

He turns to face me, a genuine, carefree smile on his face. "Ice cream sundaes."

"What?"

"We have a big decision to make, and we can't do that on an empty stomach. Serendipity 3 is down the street and I'm in the mood for a huge sundae. Let's go."

This is the easygoing Dash I'd met before. Before we slept together. Before the baby scare. The man he is around his friends and family. The one I fell for initially.

Before I can think that through, he grabs my hand again and I let him lead me along the sidewalk to the restaurant. The inside is well lit. Small white tiles, brightly colored Tiffany-styled chandeliers, pastel colors on the walls, and turquoise tabletops serve as the décor. Utterly whimsical. And I appreciate the lighter side of Dash that inspired him to come here.

There is no doubt he's famous. Even in jeans and a solid black tee, he has presence and commands a room, but nobody here recognizes him for now.

We're seated at a table, and he holds out my chair before settling himself in the one beside, not across from, me. He leans back against the chair, long legs stretched out. With a slight scruff of beard and those piercing sky-blue eyes with pinpricks of black sprinkled through, he is the epitome of sexy. I want nothing more than to straddle him where he sits, but he's made his feelings for me quite clear. He has none, other than guilt for treating me badly. And I don't want anything to do with the playboy. No matter what my body is telling me.

Needing a minute, I pick up a menu and look through the choices. "Are you eating lunch first and then dessert?" I ask him.

"Nope. Pure *decadence* for me." His eyes twinkle with amusement at his deliberate choice of words. "But feel free to order food first."

"Decadence sounds perfect." I shake my head at myself for getting into sensual word games with the man. "I mean, you're right. A time like this calls for ice cream."

"Glad we're on the same page."

A waitress stops at our table. "Hi, folks. Are you ready to order or do you need … more … time?" Her voice trails off and her eyes grow wide as she obviously recognizes Dash.

"Cass?" Dash asks, calling me by the shortened name he'd used *that* night.

I swallow hard. "I'm ready to order."

The waitress pulls herself together, obviously having been instructed to behave around celebrity guests. She politely waits.

My choice is easy. "I'll have the Forbidden Broadway Sundae."

Chocolate blackout cake, vanilla ice cream, and hot fudge topped with whipped cream. My stomach rumbles with delight at the thought. That thought of the treat bolsters my nerves when deciding what to do about Naomi's proposition.

"I'll have the same thing." He winks at me and I frown.

"What are you up to?" I narrow my gaze at him. "The word play, the winking. You won't get anywhere trying to charm me into being your pretend girlfriend, you know."

What I've come to think of as his fake smile slips. "It's a habit."

"Well, break it when I'm around. If I'm even going to consider this ludicrous plan, I want to be around someone real. Not a rock star with a massive ego he wants to project to the world."

He nods and I'm shocked he doesn't rear back at my insult.

"You know that's one of the things I like about you," he says.

"What's that?"

"You don't take my bullshit." He shrugs. "The only other people who treat me like a regular guy are my family. It's refreshing."

"Glad I can surprise you. Now tell me. Are you seriously considering this plan?" Because to my surprise, I'm considering saying yes. Axel has always been there for me, and if acting the part will help not just Dash but the group as a whole, I'll do it.

Dash blows out a long breath, picks up a spoon, and twirls it around. "I hate either of us being pushed into a situation we don't want."

"Wow. Tell me how you really feel." I swallow over the sudden lump in my throat. "You don't want to be my boyfriend, real, fake, or otherwise. Got it."

He blinks, drawing my attention to those long, fringed lashes any woman would kill to have. "Dammit, that's not how I meant it." He leans closer so only I can hear.

Unfortunately for me, the scent of his cologne is potent and arousing, and I squirm in my seat. This man is the whole package, and it isn't fair to average people walking the earth.

"At first I thought Naomi was nuts, but the more I think about it, I realize she has a point. Which is why she's paid the big bucks to come up with solutions when one of us gets into shit. And let's face it. I've gotten myself into a pretty deep hole. One I want to get out of."

He looks around and slides his arm behind me as he speaks. "I'm tired of the life I've been living. I don't want to wake up hungover or, worse, still drunk. I hate the groupies and don't want strange women pawing me. I want to focus on my music, my family, and my future."

I study him up close, stunned by his admission. "Dash Kingston wants a normal life?"

"As close to normal as I can get knowing I have to be on the road at times. But yeah. Why is that so surprising?" He hasn't moved, and his warm breath fans my ear as he talks, making it difficult for me to concentrate.

"Because you're you? A rock star who can't stand to be in the same room the morning after with a woman you slept with the night before? Does that sound normal to you?" I'm obviously still hurt. So sue me. I'm human.

"I'm sorry for that and I will make it up to you." He tucks a strand of hair behind my ear that must have fallen from my ponytail, causing a ripple of awareness to cascade through me. "Despite me being a complete asshole, I'm still asking if you'll do this for me. Be my girlfriend."

Between his nearness, his masculine, sexy scent, and the warmth of his body, my nipples grow tight, as if they're saying yes even as every other part of my body screams *no. Don't be an idiot.* I'm too susceptible to this man's charms, which means he'll hurt me again. I just know it.

But I understand why the charade is necessary, and if I can remember it's just pretend, I'll be fine. My brother just joined the band, and if they can get past this rocky period, he'll have another chance at a career with a massively successful band. We've always looked out for one another, and despite his wariness about me being Dash's so-called girlfriend, I'm an adult who makes my own decisions.

"There are some ground rules you have to agree to before I say yes," I say.

"Name them."

I sit up straighter in my chair. "One, no cheating. I don't care that we're fake," I say, whispering the word. "The world will think it's real, and I refuse to be made a fool of."

"Agreed," he says, too easily.

I narrow my eyes. "That means celibacy, in case you aren't thinking things through," I whisper.

He angles even closer. "I've been celibate since our night together. Next rule?"

What. The. Fuck?

With his thumb, he pushes my chin upward, closing my mouth, which I didn't realize I've opened in surprise. Now isn't the time to dissect that statement or even decide if I believe him.

I attempt to unscramble my brain and get to my next rule. "When we break up, I get to be the one who dumps you. Again, I won't be humiliated."

"Deal." Again, no hesitation.

Before I can try and come up with another rule to cover my ass, the waitress arrives with our sundaes. "Here you go."

Dash straightens and waits while she places our desserts in front of us. The huge metal bowl contains way too many scoops of vanilla ice cream on top of the chocolate blackout cake and so much whipped cream I'll be digging to get to the cake.

"Wow." I pick up the cherry on top and pop it into my mouth, close my lips, and pull out the stem. "Mmm." I close my eyes for a brief moment because I love cherries, and when I open them, a heavy-lidded Dash is staring back at me, desire in his gaze.

Desire I recognize, having seen that look on his face once before, which leads to my final rule. "I know we have to do PDA, but we are not sleeping together again."

An amused smile lifts his lips. "Unless you change

your mind and give me permission."

Arrogant man. And isn't that part of his appeal? "I won't," I insist.

Ignoring him, I take the long spoon and dig into the decadent dessert, shoving a huge scoop into my mouth because I don't want to discuss this subject anymore.

CHAPTER THREE

Dash

NORMALLY ONCE I'M in Manhattan, I stay in my apartment instead of heading back to the Hamptons. It's a long trip to do twice in one day, especially with traffic, but Cassidy has rented a house near Xander and Sasha's, and she has nowhere to stay in the city. She could sleep at my place in a guest room, but I already know she'd refuse.

I don't want to send her back to the beach alone, and since she is technically my assistant, at least for now, I ask her to call a car service to take us home. I'm not in the mood to deal with an Uber driver who might be a fan. The service the band uses knows better than to bother their clients.

Since the waitress has been so good about giving us space, privacy, and anonymity, I leave her an extra-large tip. I hear her mention to another server that her son loves the guitar and is a fan, so I ask her the kid's name, sign a personal note, and leave it along with the gratuity.

I notice Cassidy's soft expression, but I'm not doing it to win points. I'm grateful for them as I need her to relax around me, but the truth is, I like to show my appreciation to people who treat me like a regular human being and not a famous star they want something from.

We drive back to East Hampton in silence, and I sense Cassidy was thinking about what she's gotten herself into by agreeing to be my fake girlfriend. Hell, I'm wondering the same thing. But there's something about this woman that affects me and has from the moment I saw her for the first time. I'm not a romantic, not by a long shot, but one look at her porcelain skin, delicate nose, full lips, jade eyes I could get lost in, and I felt a connection. One I was smart enough to act on and stupid enough to not treat with care.

I ask the driver to stop at Cassidy's first. She's rented a pretty Cape Cod house, small by East Hampton standards, but the whole look of the place, from the colorful flowers out front to the rocking bench on the porch, suits her.

While the driver waits, I walk her to the door, pausing as she opens her bag and looks for her keys, which she fishes out after a solid minute of rooting around.

"So are you sure you're good with the plan?" I ask before she can unlock her door.

She nods. "I'm sure." As she is about to slide the

key into the lock, I slip an arm around her waist and turn her to face me.

She jerks at my touch and pulls back. "What are you doing?"

"Making a point." And crowding her because I want to. "If we're going to make people believe our relationship is real, you can't flinch every time I get close."

She closes her eyes and sighs. "I know that, and in public I'll be fine."

I place my knuckle under her chin, forcing her to meet my gaze. "What if a photographer is hiding and watching now?" I doubt it, but I want her to understand what us *being in a relationship* means.

Her eyes open wide at my question. I don't hesitate. I lean in and brush my lips over hers, letting my mouth settle where it belongs. She stiffens in shock, but I keep up the connection, sliding my lips along hers, and in seconds she melts against me, accepting what I offer.

Touching her, our mouths melding, I find the very thing that scared me off the first time. Peace. But I've learned my lesson and I'm not about to run off again.

I have her. I could slip my tongue inside and up the heat factor. God knows I want to but I've made my point. We still have chemistry, and she needs to accept my public displays of affection whenever I offer them if we are going to pull off this charade. I already know, the minute I leave her alone, she'll beat herself up and second-guess every second of this kiss. No need to push her harder. I have time for that.

I lift my mouth and touch my forehead to hers, catching my breath and letting her come to her senses. "See? That's the way to act around me."

As I expected, she stiffens, but nobody is around to notice. I press a kiss to her nose and take a step back. "Go inside. I'll check in later about our schedule."

She's obviously too dazed by our kiss to lecture me, and thank God for small favors. My dick throbs in my pants, and all I want to do is get home and jerk off so I can concentrate on what comes next with my new *girlfriend*.

She does as I ask and steps into her house, slamming the door hard behind her without even a goodbye.

Grinning, I jog back to the limousine, not thrown by her behavior. I have her off-balance. Wanting me one minute, furious at me the next. I can work with that.

Because one thing I've come to realize: I don't want Cassidy to be my *fake* anything. I've fucked up too badly to try and convince her otherwise now. But with this so-called charade my publicist has thought up, I have a second chance to show her the man I can be now that I understand what I want.

The driver takes me home, and I head straight to the shower to wash off the grime of the city. Maybe I'm more like Xander than I thought, enjoying the solitude of the Hamptons…when the guys aren't partying, that is.

I tip my head back and let the spray of the shower wash over me. After cleaning up with soap, I clasp my cock in my hand, tighten my grip, and groan, pumping my hand up and down my shaft, all the while thinking of Cassidy.

I sat beside her for the better part of today, inhaling her warm, exotic scent that always arouses me as I remember taking her in the hotel bed many times and in a variety of positions.

I lean back against the marble wall, arousal flowing like lava through my veins as I work my dick with one hand.

At the hotel, I'd started on top and come so hard I thought I was done for the night. I'd eaten her out as I thankfully recovered, then flipped her so she could ride me, her warm, wet walls clenching around me. Making me wish for the first time ever I hadn't needed to use anything between us.

At the thought, my balls draw up, I work myself faster, and I come hard, my semen coating the shower walls and floor. I shake my head and give myself a few minutes before grabbing the hand-held shower head and rinsing off the evidence.

This is becoming routine considering I wasn't kidding when I told Cassidy I've been celibate since that night with her. I am aware I shocked her with that news. I know she doesn't believe me and though I wish otherwise, I'll have to work on convincing her I'm telling the truth. Oh, there've been groupies at parties since who have come on to me, but my dick remains limp. The only time I get hard is when I think about my new fake girlfriend.

For a while, I had the paternity accusation to deal with, and that's enough to make any guy want to steer clear of casual sex, but it isn't just that and I know it.

It has been four days since I've known for sure I wasn't going to be a father, and I've spent that time alone. The guys live with me and that's fine, but I've stayed holed up in my room, eating at odd times when nobody will be around or going to Xander's and hanging out at his pool, where peace and quiet surround me.

I needed the time to think. About how I have been an asshole in so many ways. Yes, the rock star lifestyle gives me perks and lets me believe I'm special, but my family keeps me grounded, treating me no differently just because of my fame. Until I was accused of fathering a child with some chick I can barely remember, and then they all started tiptoeing around me.

The days I spent at Xander's were enlightening. Watching my brother and Sasha together leaves me feeling envious, something I've never experienced before around my coupled siblings. Xander and Sasha's ease with each other, the way they take care of one another, the happiness in my brother's eyes makes even a cynic like me take notice. Especially since I've had my eyes opened to the stupid, selfish way I've been living my life.

I think about Xander's path to where he is now. He'd enlisted in the Marines rather than follow Linc's footsteps in the family business. He'd wanted to get away from our father, Kenneth, and his cheating bullshit and unrealistic expectations. When he'd bothered to pay attention to his children, that was.

With Kenneth dead and gone for a while now, thanks to a heart attack, our family has been able to relax. Sad but true. But Xander didn't come home from Afghanistan the same kid he was before being medically discharged thanks to an injury from his proximity to an IED. Xander became darker, quieter, and more solitary.

Until Sasha came back into his life. Working through their issues and dealing with her stalker hasn't been easy, but I can see now it was worth it. They're forgetting their past and focusing on their future, and I see the difference Sasha makes and how much lighter and happier my sibling is now.

Then there is Linc. My oldest brother, who takes everyone's problems on his shoulders, including finding the sister we knew nothing about until our dad's death. With Jordan, his personal assistant and best friend, by his side, they'd followed leads, found Aurora, brought her into the family fold, and in the process, Linc and Jordan had discovered they were soul mates.

I was with Linc this weekend, but did I ask how my niece is doing? How Jordan is feeling? No, because I'm a dick, worried about my own problems and letting my brothers dance around me while I stewed and waited for the test results.

Even my sister, Chloe, who had been jilted at the altar and rescued by Linc's nemesis, Beck Daniels, is now engaged and living with the man she loves. But again, I've been too wrapped up in myself to check in with my sister.

I hadn't been kidding Cassidy when I said I want to change my lifestyle. I want to be someone my family can be proud of and a woman like Cassidy would want to be with.

I have my work cut out for me.

Cassidy

FROM THE MINUTE I enter my house, I can't relax. What was I thinking, agreeing to be Dash's fake girlfriend? For a playboy like him, I might as well have given him an all-clear. He kissed me, and I'd melted into him like any good groupie would have. And let's face it, he treated me no better than one the only time we were together.

But he's right. I do have to acclimate to being around him, letting him touch me, and reciprocating in an easy, casual manner. Without falling for him further in the process. I need someone to talk to, but I don't want to bother Sasha or take her away from Xander.

Which explains why, instead of working, I bake cookies from scratch, using the recipe my grandmother taught me when she treated us to dessert for high grades or good behavior. The delicious smell permeates my nostrils, making my stomach grumble.

Once they cool, I intend to binge a television show and indulge. This will be my second treat today, the first being the ice cream sundae. Three if I include Dash's kiss.

Dammit. I shake my head at my thoughts and stride from the kitchen to the family room in my quaint rental home. I fell in love with the place at first sight, I think, as I settle into the cushy sofa I purchased for comfort rather than looks.

Working for Sasha over the past four years, the last two being extremely lucrative as my friend's career soars, I can afford to live in a larger home on East Hampton. But after a childhood of not having much and refusing to live off my brother's money after he made it big with Caged Chaos, I want to save what I earn.

I'd only agreed to live with Sasha in her huge LA mansion after insisting on paying something in rent despite my friend wanting me to just move in and accept her generosity. I didn't grow up with a lot, but I've always had my pride. And I intend to hang on to the security my current financial situation offers.

My doorbell rings and I rise, walking to the entry and finding my brother on the other side. I let him in. "Hey, Ax."

"Cass." He pulls me in for a hug, and I wrap my arms around him to reciprocate. "I smell Grandma's cookies," he says.

I laugh as he releases me and starts for the kitchen. "Leave it to you to show up when they're ready."

"Got milk?" he asks as he enters the room.

I head to the refrigerator and pour us each a glass. We sit on the small barstools around the center island.

He grabs the top cookie from the pile and takes a huge bite. "You've got the magic touch. Grandma taught you well."

I smile, thinking about the woman who'd taken us in, no questions asked. "That she did." I prop my chin on my hands. "I miss her."

"Me, too." He downs half of his milk, places the glass on the counter, and meets my gaze. "Okay, why'd you agree?"

I don't have to wonder what he is referring to. He was obviously home when Dash had returned, and he'd probably filled them all in on me agreeing to be his fake girlfriend.

"Because Naomi's reasons made sense. If Dash and his offstage women and antics disappear, the press will turn their attention to your music and how well you fit into the band. And that's what you need right now." I put my hand on his. "I did it for you."

He shakes his head. "There were other ways. We didn't brainstorm them yet, but I'm certain we can figure one out. Everyone knows what a man-whore Dash is. I don't want you getting involved with him."

I frown, uncomfortable with his description of Dash, despite having thought it myself. Which reminds me of something Dash said earlier today. *I've been celibate since our night together.*

I shiver and wonder if he'd been telling me the

truth. I doubt he'd lie, but I have a hunch his reasons for not having sex have more to do with being scared to death he'd impregnated that woman than because of his feelings for *me*.

I refocus on my bossy brother. "You're speaking like it's your decision. It's not. It's mine. And after all you've done for me over the years, helping Grandma, taking care of me, I need to step up for you."

I refuse to say another word about it. I've made my choice. I pick up a cookie and split it in half, the gooey chocolate still melting. I take a bite and reach for a napkin, wiping my face.

"Stop staring at me," I mutter.

"You're a stubborn pain in the ass."

I'm tempted to stick out my tongue like when we were kids. "Can't you just let me do what I need to do without giving me a hard time?"

He nods but a small grumble escapes from his throat. "I'm just used to looking out for you."

"I appreciate it but it's also time to let me live my life." I hesitate. "And make my own mistakes."

He stiffens his body and narrows his gaze. "What does that mean? What did you do?"

For half a second, I consider telling him about my night with Dash but immediately change my mind. No way will I do anything to cause a fight between him and his lead singer. "Nothing. Relax. I'm just saying back off."

Axel snatches another cookie. "Fine. But be smart."

I roll my eyes. "Aren't I always?"

He rises and yanks on my ponytail. "Thanks for the cookies."

I stand. "That's it? You just came to give me the third degree?"

He nods. "That's what brothers are for. Love you, Cass."

"Love you, too." I start walking him to the door. "Oh, wait. Take some cookies!" I rush back to the kitchen and pack up a bunch for him to bring home, then I let him out and lock up behind him.

After heading back to the kitchen, I clean up our snack, cover the cookies so they don't get stale, and decide I'm not in the mood to binge watch any shows.

Instead, I take a long, hot bath, during which I force myself to put my concerns out of my mind and let myself enjoy and relax. Later, wearing my favorite old tee shirt, I sit down on my bed and pull out my laptop to go over scheduling.

I already know the biggest night this week is Sunday. The band will be performing at the MTV Video Music Awards at the Barclays Center in Brooklyn. The limousines are booked. The guys have spent plenty of time practicing and have to be at the arena on

Wednesday for rehearsal.

Emails have piled up during the day, and I scan through the ones from the band's label to add dates to the calendar, following them up with cc'd emails to the guys, letting them know where they have to be and when.

Then I settle in to read, but despite my best effort to concentrate, all I can think about is Dash and that kiss.

I WAKE UP the next morning to another glorious sunrise. Given the time of year, the days of warm temperatures are numbered. Taking advantage while I can, I step onto my small back patio, cup of coffee in hand. I don't have a beach view, but I enjoy the grass and the trees surrounding me, and the peace and quiet outside.

I hear the doorbell and sigh. "Peace and quiet broken," I grumble, wondering who could be visiting so early. At least I'm showered and dressed for the day and not still in my nightshirt.

I glance through the peephole, narrowing my eyes at my unexpected company. I open the door to Naomi and the band's manager, Dean Jerome. Both dressed like savvy New Yorkers, Dean in slim European-cut pants, dress shirt and jacket, and an expensive haircut, Naomi in her designer dress and heels. They make me feel like a country bumpkin in my floral summer dress.

Worse, Dean and I have been like oil and water from the first day we met when he'd tracked Dash down at Xander's. I was still working for Sasha at the time. I brought the man a drink, tripped and spilled it on his white dress shirt, and the tone of our relationship was set.

It doesn't help that he rubs me the wrong way. His arrogance and lack of respect for what the band wants infuriates her. And since he treats me like a servant, I refuse to bend to his will on principle. Just because I'm the band's assistant doesn't make me less human than his royal highness.

And then there was the time Dean came over to meet with the band not long after their original drummer had quit but Axel was already in talks to join them. I had been present because Dash had invited Xander over. Xander brought Sasha and Sasha insisted I join them. Typical Kingston gathering.

Dean and the band hadn't excused themselves to be alone for the conversation, and Dean had pulled up a demo of another drummer for the guys to see and hear. A young up-and-coming musician whose background came from more of a blues sound than the Original Kings' indie/alternative rock feel. I didn't think he fit with the vibe of the band. I'd glanced around the table to gauge their interest. Mac was frowning. Jagger's gaze was narrowed. And Dash had a blank expression on his face. Xander, Linc, and Sasha remained silent, but I, who'd grown up around my brother's talent, had blurted out my opinion.

Though I hadn't wanted my brother, who was already invested, to get screwed over, I also thought my standpoint was valid. So had Dash. And just as I'd sensed, the rest of the band agreed, making me the source of Dean's always-present anger.

Now he stands on my doorstep with Naomi.

"Well, this is a surprise. Are you sure you don't have the wrong house?" I ask, unsure why they've shown up here at this hour.

"Actually, we'd like to talk to *you*," Naomi says with a smile. The band's publicist has always been pleasant and nice, so I have no issue with her. Other than the fact that Naomi had volunteered me to be Dash's girlfriend. But she could have called before just showing up, I think.

Dean doesn't appear to be in a friendly mood, but what else is new? He stands there, looking me over, a scowl on his face, and clearly finding me lacking.

"Come in." I step aside so they can enter. "Can I get you coffee, water…?" What do you offer people at nine thirty a.m.?

"We're good, thanks. Can we sit?" Naomi asks.

"Sure." I lead them to the small living room, and we settle into seats.

At least Naomi and I do. Dean leans against the wall and glances at his phone before meeting my gaze.

"Why do I feel like the kid in the principal's office about to be lectured?" I ask.

Dean pushes himself off the wall. "Naomi told me about her idea for you and Dash to pretend to be in a relationship. Dash called last night, all excited about it, but frankly, I don't think it's the right move."

Naomi scowls at him.

I straighten my shoulders, refusing to be intimidated. "Why aren't you discussing this with Dash?"

"Because I thought you'd be more reasonable. What Dash doesn't understand is that any publicity is good publicity. So what if his social life is the subject of interviews? As long as the band is in the spotlight, it doesn't matter why."

"I disagree," Naomi says.

Dean scowls. "Dash pays you to do what he wants. I'm thinking of the overall good of the band."

I rise to my feet. "Again, why are you trying to convince me? This is Dash's life. It's his choice how he wants to handle things."

"Yes, but you can say no. Honestly, do you think the world is going to believe that Dash Kingston fell for the girl next door?" He waves a hand at me dismissively. "He'd be better off making a deal with an A-lister like Sasha or a young model."

I glare at him. "That was rude. And you don't need to make excuses for why you don't want me in the role. We both know you don't like me." *And the feeling is mutual*, I think. "But I don't have to listen to your insults in my home."

"I told you to stay in the car," Naomi mutters. "Cassidy, you know this was my idea, so I support you. I came to make sure you would feel comfortable in Dash's world. I thought maybe we could go shopping so you have the right clothes for the VMAs and the after-parties."

I blink, surprised that Naomi is taking this asshole's side on anything. "Just because I dress casually at home doesn't mean I don't know how to make an impression at an event. I assumed you'd know that or why suggest me for the role?"

These two people don't pay my salary, the band does, and I'm playing girlfriend at Dash's request. Though if I have to put up with this bullshit, I might rethink my answer.

"What's going on here?" Dash has let himself in through the unlocked door and stands in the entry of the room, anger emanating from him, his body vibrating with emotion.

"Dash. We were coming to see you after we stopped here," Dean says. "How did you know we were at Ms. Forrester's?"

I suppress an eye roll at his solicitous behavior toward his top client when, seconds ago, he'd been insulting me.

"Xander was taking his morning run and saw you two get out of the car. He figured I'd want to know." Dash folds his muscled arms across his chest.

In faded jeans, Vans on his feet, a tight tee shirt, and a basic pair of Ray-Ban sunglasses, he appears damned sexy and intimidating as hell.

"What are you up to?" he demands of his manager.

The man runs a hand through his slick hair. "I was trying to convince Cassidy that this relationship shit is a bad idea."

"Actually, he insinuated nobody would believe you'd fall for someone like me. He'd prefer an actress or a model." I turn to Naomi next. I'm not letting either of them off the hook. "And Naomi wants to take me clothes shopping so I don't embarrass you at the awards."

"What the fuck?" Dash glares at them both.

"I'm just saying all publicity is good publicity. So what if they're talking about you escaping a baby scare? It keeps the band in the news." Dean's face turns red beneath his tan.

"It should be about the music and Axel, our new band member. Naomi's right. If I'm in a relationship, they'll find me boring in no time and discuss what matters. Decision made and I don't want to hear another word about it." Dash stands up to his manager, and yeah, I find that hot, too.

"Fine," Dean mutters.

I can't let Naomi's insinuation that I'm some girl who can't handle myself in an upscale world stand. "Naomi, would you like to check out the designer clothes in my closet? I did live in LA and I worked for Sasha Keaton. I've been to the Oscars. I think I can handle dressing for the music awards."

The other woman lets out a sigh. "I'm sorry. I let this one get to me on the ride here." She jerks a finger toward Dean.

Dash walks across the room and puts an arm around me, taking me off guard. "I think the question is, why would a woman like *this* fall for a man like me?" He lets his words drop hard before continuing. "Now, if you two are finished sticking your noses where they don't belong, it's time for you to leave."

I blink and a lump rises in my throat at his unexpected, protective defense.

"I'll be right back," he says, pressing a kiss to my forehead that doesn't appear to be for show.

He walks them out to the car, and through the

window, I see Dash get into it with Dean. Finally, Dash spins away and stomps back to the house, hands clenched in tight fists.

I meet him in the front hall. "Is everything okay?"

"No. I'm fucking pissed off. They had no right to come at you like that."

I sigh. "I handled them."

"But you shouldn't have had to. And they had no right to make you feel like you weren't up to some nonexistent set of standards," he says, his voice low and still angry.

I bite down on my lower lip. "Actually, they had a point and I need to call Sasha."

"What are you talking about?" he asks.

"I lied. I never went to the Oscars and I didn't even think about having the right kind of clothes to be seen on a rock star's arm. Sasha and I need to go shopping." I shrug, doing my best not to show my embarrassment.

His laughter takes me by surprise and lightens the mood.

"What? I wasn't going to admit to Naomi or Dean that they had made any kind of point."

Dash takes two steps toward me and braces my face in his hands. "Cassidy Forrester, you are one of a kind. I mean that in the best possible way, so don't let anyone try and convince you otherwise."

I tip my head back, and as he looks into my eyes, his lips come down on mine. With nobody watching, no chance of being photographed, he treats me to the softest, most sensual kiss of my life.

His lips are smooth and take me to another place. One where only we exist. Desire sweeps through me, and I rub my body against his, soaking up his heat and inhaling his scent. His tongue swirls against mine, and I moan into his mouth, my need ramping up with every brush of his tongue.

With a rumbling groan, he breaks the kiss. I expect a satisfied grin, but when I open my eyes, his gaze is hazy, his smile genuine.

"I meant what I said. You're better than me, Cass. You don't need new clothes to make a point. But since I know you'll feel better if you go shopping, use my credit card. It's a business expense," he says before I can argue.

He slides his hand into his pocket, pulls out his wallet, and places a black card on the credenza. "Call me if they give you a hard time."

He starts for the door and I can't hold it in. "Dash?"

"Yeah?"

What can I say? *Why did you kiss me when there was no one watching?*

He's confusing me and I need space to build my walls.

I shake my head. "Never mind. It's nothing."

He narrows his gaze, studying me. "I don't want to rush and fuck things up again. I'll be in touch, Cass."

And with that disconcerting statement, he turns and walks out the door.

I shake off his words and go looking for my cell, dialing my best friend, the woman who knows how to do glam better than anyone else I know.

When it comes to his new *girlfriend*, Dash is in for the shock of a lifetime.

★   ★   ★

Dash

I STEP OUTSIDE and shut Cassidy's door, uncertainty nagging me as I head to my car, parked on the street in front of her house. All I can think about are those sweet lips tipped upward, her eyes half-mast, her lashes dark against her pale skin. And her taste? I'll be attempting to put those feelings into lyrics and then to music because it was too beautiful not to memorialize in song.

But the physical is easy. I ought to know, given how many women I've had in my bed. None of them ever mattered.

Cassidy does and I need her to know that I'm not

jumping in because she's another easy body available to me. I need to show her I am *in*.

I run a hand through my hair as I climb into my car and begin my short ride home. Proving myself to Cassidy begins with backing her up when my team oversteps. I'm still livid with my manager for how he'd treated Cass. As for Naomi, though she means well, she'd handled things wrong, too. I let them both know it when I walked them to the town car they'd shared for the ride from the city. A driver was waiting for them in the air-conditioned vehicle, of course.

I'll be damned if I'm going to let Dean throw his weight around in an attempt to intimidate Cassidy because he doesn't like a decision I made or the woman I chose. My manager is a publicity hound, and he doesn't care what form the mention comes in as long as the band is on someone's radar. Anything that keeps us relevant and makes him and the label money. At one time, I didn't care about interview content either, but my views have changed, and Dean needs to respect my decisions. More importantly, he has to respect Cassidy.

I pull into my driveaway, climb out of the car and walk inside, not surprised to find Axel waiting for me when I enter through the front door.

He was in the kitchen making a smoothie when Xander had called with the news that our manager and publicist were at Cassidy's. And I had been stupid enough to put my phone on speaker.

I'm just lucky Axel didn't come with me. The man would have taken two seconds to figure out I'm interested in his sister, and that can only lead to trouble.

"Hey." I toss my keys into a metal dish I keep on the credenza.

"How'd it go?" Axel folds his arms across his chest.

If anyone can understand being protective of a sister, it's me. I'd be just as worked up if anyone went after Chloe or Aurora.

"Dean was being an asshole," I say. "I handled it, but for what it's worth, Cassidy had it under control before I walked in. She wasn't taking his shit, and that should make it easier for her to deal with him going forward. He won't think he can push her around."

Axel nods, pride in his gaze. "That's Cass. Never did let people tell her what to do. But I don't like the fact that she's involved in your personal life."

"So you've said but I suggest you get used to it." I have no intention of explaining that my personal feelings are involved.

Axel narrows his eyes but treats me to a curt nod, which I take to mean the other man won't cause trouble within the band, but he'll keep an eye on me when it comes to his sister.

Fair enough.

"Ready to head to rehearsal?" I ask. We'll be spending the rest of the day in my soundproof studio going over the tracks we're performing at Sunday night's show.

Axel pulls his drumsticks from his back pocket. "We've got a show to do."

And a red carpet to walk, with interviews, as we make our way backstage. I blow out a breath, telling myself Cassidy can handle herself in front of a live audience. Our first time in public as a couple.

Talk about throwing her into the deep end. I console myself with the fact that I'll be by her side, there to catch her if she stumbles. But the more I get to know her, the more I realize Cassidy will always fake it before letting the world know there's a soft core inside. One that is capable of being hurt, something I've done to her once already, and have no plans to do again.

CHAPTER FOUR

Dash

I SIT WITH Xander in my brother's family room, waiting for the women, who are busy with their glam squad in the master bedroom, getting ready for tonight's event. Sasha has scored an invite as a presenter at the VMAs and that lets me hang with my brother. Even better, it gives Cass a friend to keep her calm.

She hasn't said a word, but I've noticed how uptight she's been all throughout the week as we ease into public life, and a lot of that is my fault because I've insinuated myself into her life. On purpose.

I've started taking her out, small trips into town for coffee, wearing our most casual clothing, sunglasses, walking hand in hand. I'm known as a local, and though many people give me privacy, tourists are more likely to take photos and post my whereabouts.

On the surface, that is exactly what I want. A slow lead-in to tonight's red carpet walk that will make us an official couple in the eyes of the world. I'm hoping for a burst of excitement that will quickly die down, leaving me out of the spotlight.

But that doesn't account for my behavior when we're alone. My hand around her waist. A peck on the cheek *just because*, and long, lingering good-night or goodbye kisses that could easily escalate if not for me deliberately saving my best for tonight, after the performance, when we're alone.

"You're quiet," Xander says into the silence.

I shrug. "Just thinking."

"About?" Xander adjusts his black-rimmed glasses.

"Headache?" I ask.

Xander usually wears his glasses when his eyes and head act up as a result of a concussion in an IED blast during his time as a Marine. Not easy for a man who is a writer.

"I was up late working. Vision's a little blurry. Don't change the subject," my brother says with a scowl.

Though I would rather ask Xander how he's going to deal with tonight's crowds and flashing lights, my brother won't let me avoid the conversation.

Besides, I know the occasional red carpet as a couple is one of the concessions Xander made in order to have a relationship with a famous actress. Sasha moved across the country to New York to be with him, and they're starting their production company, ending her country-hopping schedule of multiple movies a year. They love each other and are making things work.

I turn my thoughts back to Cassidy. I glance toward the part of the house where the bedrooms are located.

"I'm just hoping I didn't push her into something she's not ready for to suit my selfish needs." I rise to my feet and shove my hands into my front pants pockets.

Xander tips his head to the side and studies me. "Sasha said Cassidy is fine with the fake relationship. Are you the one with the nerves?"

I shrug. "I'm just concerned about putting her under the microscope that is my life."

Xander nods. "Considering I'm the non-famous one in my relationship with Sasha, I can relate. I can also tell you Cassidy wouldn't put herself in this position if she couldn't handle it." He leans forward. "I want you to know that I appreciate that you're looking out for her during this charade."

Xander's words get under my skin. "It's not a damned charade!" I all but explode.

"What are you saying?" Xander asks. "You already used Cassidy once. Are you telling me—"

"Whoa." I hold up one hand. "First of all, I didn't use her. She scared the crap out of me," I say, disliking the admission as it comes out of my mouth.

My brother's eyes open wide.

"And second, believe it or not, that baby scare taught me a lesson. Watching you and Sasha, Linc and Jordan, and Chloe and Beck has been eye-opening."

"Well, I'll be damned. You have real feelings for Cassidy."

Xander's shock is palpable. My brother never thought I was capable of deep emotion, and I know it's because I've never given anyone a reason to think I take the women in my life seriously.

"I do." My chest squeezes tight at the truth. "I don't think Cassidy will buy a word I say, but I'm trying to take it slow and be a better guy."

I shrug, uncomfortable in my fake leather jacket and pants, but we have a show to do on live television. I can't wear my favorite jeans with holes that are shredded at the bottom. Well, I can, but the band has voted on a more upscale look, given the opportunity.

Xander walks over and places a hand on my shoulder, squeezing tight. "You worked your ass off to get where you are, and you were entitled to have fun in the process. But I'm glad you're ready to grow up. Good luck proving yourself. If anyone deserves a chance at being happy, it's you."

I grin. "Look at us, being all sappy."

Xander slaps me on the side of the head, something he does too often.

"Hey! Watch the hair." We had a stylist at my house earlier for all the guys.

Afterward, I came to Xander's, and the band will be taking their own limo, for which I'm grateful. Lately I've begun to feel like I need more space. Treating my house like a dorm isn't working for me anymore. Another problem for another time, I think.

Cassidy's laugh sounds from the other side of the house, and my cock jerks in response.

"Ready or not, here we come!" Sasha calls out.

Both of us turn.

Sasha strides out in a silver gown, but I only have eyes for Cassidy. Unlike the A-list actress, Cassidy looks every inch the rocker's girlfriend, and I can't stop staring.

Matching me, she wears a black long-sleeve leather blazer with lace-up grommet detail and slit sides, a low vee exposing her incredible cleavage, and she's paired the jacket with black biker shorts and high-heeled booties. Her hair has been pulled into a high side ponytail, slicked back except for the long fringe hanging on one side of her face. The golden tone on her skin, along with her matching bronze-colored makeup and lips, blows me away.

She looks gorgeous and utterly fuckable.

My cock is hard as a rock, but between my black clothing and the jacket, nobody will notice if I stay that way all night.

Aware of my brother and Sasha in a huddle of their own, I step toward her, grasping her hands in mine, taking note of her new long, squared metallic-coated nails. I was drawn to her before, all facets of her looks and personality, but *this* woman is my walking wet dream.

"Holy shit, Cass." I stare into her eyes, the green color sparkling against the black backdrop of her outfit.

"You like?"

"I want to throw you over my shoulder, haul you to the nearest bed, and fuck you senseless." I blink, surprised I let those words come out.

She grins, shocking me. "I'll take that as the best kind of compliment."

"As you should."

She pats the lapel of my jacket. "Looking pretty hot yourself."

Apparently while I've been worried about Cassidy, she's been taking confidence pills. In truth, all she had to do was look in a mirror to know she'll make the right impression tonight and torture me in the process.

"Everyone ready?" Xander asks.

The limousines have been waiting outside for an hour, and since we're still ninety minutes from the city, preparation had to begin early so we could leave the

Hamptons and arrive with plenty of time to spare, even if we hit traffic.

I glance at Cassidy. "Are you set?"

She nods but I note her white knuckles as she grips a small Balenciaga handbag.

I lean in, lips near her ear. "Don't worry. I've got you." I whisper the promise.

The only time she'll be alone is during the setup and my performance, and I'll make sure she is settled with Xander before heading backstage.

Before and after, I'm all hers.

★ ★ ★

Cassidy

UTTERLY FUCKABLE. I can live with that. Just like I've been navigating the different way Dash has been treating me this past week. I'm not stupid and know his most sensual touches and kisses haven't been for show. We've been behind closed doors and I've allowed each one. If his goal has been to breach my physical walls, it's worked. I go to sleep each night with the memory of his taste on my lips and his touch causing my body to tingle.

But if he's been hoping to tear down the emotional barriers I put up after he walked out on me last time, he's doomed to disappointment. I already had Adam dump me because he didn't like the long-distance relationship my job had forced us to be in. I keep telling myself he didn't hurt me, and because we've been so busy dealing with Sasha's stalker, movie, and move, I've been able to bury my emotions and focus on other things. But the fact remains that the man I'd been in a serious relationship with dumped me over a text message.

Then Dash swept into my life, and for a few short days, he took it over. He was with me at the hospital when I was injured after being mistaken for Sasha by the man stalking her, and he'd seemed worried about me afterwards. And when Sasha and I needed help, Dash had been there, leading to our night in bed. We absolutely have a connection. One I've never felt before. But like Adam, Dash left me alone. Without warning, disappearing from my life in any meaningful way.

Suffice it to say, I'm wary of men in general and Dash specifically. I've been hurt more by him than Adam, and that's enough of a warning not to let him in again.

But that doesn't mean I won't appreciate being his girlfriend in public, and if he wants to sleep with me during the course of this charade, why not enjoy that, too? Something I decided between my glam experience and walking out to see the approval in Dash's expressive eyes. As long as I keep my heart locked up tight during our temporary affair, I'll be fine. Because clearly that's where this is headed.

For the ride to and from the city, I booked a deluxe limousine for me, Dash, Xander and Sasha, but when I step outside to find two vehicles waiting, I stop in my tracks.

"I don't understand." I reach for my small bag to retrieve my phone and call the company when Dash places a hand over mine.

"I changed the reservation." He inclines his head at his brother. "We'll see you there."

Xander grins, Sasha laughs, and they head for their own vehicle.

"Why did you book two cars?" I ask.

"So we could be alone." He places a hand on my lower back, and a current of electricity buzzes along my spine as he leads me to where the driver stands, back door open.

I slide into the seat and Dash joins me.

When the door slams shut, he turns to face me. "I appreciate you doing this for me. Especially tonight. I know it's not easy, but I'm not going to abandon you to the wolves."

"I'm honestly okay. I can't say I'm looking forward to the red carpet walk, but once that's over, my nerves will calm down."

His hand covers mine, and he smooths his fingers over my knuckles. "You'll wow them."

I roll my eyes. "They're there to see you."

"Well, they're getting *us*." He leans back and relaxes, and I follow suit.

The trip to the city is quiet, and we don't encounter any more traffic than expected. The sun has already dipped low on the horizon when the limousine nears the venue. My stomach is in knots. The wait for our car to reach its ultimate destination feels endless.

Dash holds on to my hand. The pad of his thumb soothing in a rhythmic motion over my skin is meant to calm me, but nothing can. Not until I've made this long walk without tripping or making a fool of myself in front of television cameras.

"Ready?" Dash asks as our car door is opened for us.

I nod. "As I'll ever be," I mutter.

He steps out and holds out his hand, helping me as I try to delicately exit the limousine. My heart pounds in my chest as we approach the red carpet, and suddenly I'm bombarded by flashing lights and questions being called out.

Dash grasps my palm firmly in his as we make the long walk, stopping occasionally for posed shots, and he takes full advantage of the media, wrapping an arm around my waist and pulling me close. I do my best to fake it, cozying up to him, placing my hand on his chest, and smiling the whole time.

The MTV host, a beautiful woman, also glammed up, stops us to talk. "Dash, you've never walked the carpet with a woman on your arm before."

"That's because I've never found one worth it before." He turns to me and treats me to a smile filled with genuine warmth. Not the one I've come to think of as his stage grin.

Warning myself to remember this is for show, I look at him with adoration, but I'm still taken off guard when he braces his hands on my waist and pulls me close. He presses his lips to mine in what I'd call a fun kiss, one definitely done to make a point to those watching. But the way he looks at me makes it hard to remember we aren't a real couple.

"So you're Cassidy Forrester, Axel Forrester's sister," the woman says.

Dash's publicist has dropped the official news about his current relationship in time for tonight's event.

"I am," I say with a smile.

"I think a lot of women are wishing they were you right now," the host says, her comment not catty but genuine.

I'm about to answer when Dash lets out a low

chuckle. "I'm a changed man," he says, kissing the top of my hand that's still joined with his.

"We already saw the band. They seem ready to perform. Especially Axel. Have you all gelled?"

"You'll have to wait and see." Dash winks at her and soon we're walking again.

Somehow, we make it the rest of the way down the red carpet, and when I step off, I'm able to breathe once more.

"Cass!"

Sasha's voice rings out and I turn to my friend. "I made it!" I say, laughing.

Sasha, Xander beside her, pulls me into a hug. "I bet you looked amazing on TV."

I shudder at the thought, well aware the camera isn't always flattering. "I'd rather not see for myself."

"She was amazing." Dash puts his hand on my back. Chills I'm growing used to when he touches me ripple along my spine. "I'm going to leave you in good hands," he says. "I'll catch up with you after our set. But first…"

I raise my eyebrows.

"I need a kiss for good luck." Before I can respond, he leans in and presses his lips to mine, and it is no quick kiss. He slides his tongue past my parted lips and brands me with long, deep strokes that leave me panting.

By the time he lifts his head, his breathing is heavy, too. "See you soon."

Dazed, I manage a nod, and he leaves, giving off superstar vibes as he walks away.

"Umm, wow. That was not a *for show* kiss," Sasha says, speaking low. "What do you have to say for yourself?"

I blink in an attempt to refocus on my surroundings.

"I honestly don't know. This is how he's been acting for the last week."

"Even when you're alone?" Sasha asks.

I nod.

"And you're letting him back in?" she asks, her worry etched on her face.

"No. Not that way. Just … I'll make the status of our relationship clear to him when tonight's over. But can we not discuss this here? Or in front of *him*?" I tip my head toward Sasha's fiancé, and she nods in understanding.

Xander stands by her side, quiet as he deals with the lights, the noise around us, and no doubt the concert to come. I know what it takes for him to be here tonight. He's wound tight, but he's put the woman he loves first. And I admit, if only to myself, that as happy as I am for Sasha, I yearn for someone to care that deeply for me one day.

A glance at Sasha tells me she's now staring at Xander, too. "Are you okay?" she asks him.

He nods. "I'm fine, sunshine. Don't worry."

A warmth settles in my heart at the tender way Xander both speaks to and gazes at Sasha, who looks gorgeous. Her blond hair has been pulled back in a chic Old Hollywood-style bun, soft tendrils falling around her face. Her silver gown's sparkle is in no need of expensive jewels. The man hovering nearby is enough of an accessory.

And very silent as he's listening to us speak, leading me to wonder what Xander knows about his brother's sudden change in behavior toward me. And why Dash is consistently acting like the doting boyfriend when all he needs to do is put on a public display now and again.

"I think it's time to take our seats," Xander says.

Sasha nods. "Since I'm presenting early in the evening, I'm going backstage. You two be good." She presses a kiss to Xander's lips and whispers something in his ear.

"Good luck out there," I say.

Sasha grins. "Piece of cake."

And for her, being a talented actress, it is.

She strides away, stopping to talk to people she knows on her way. Famous people. Though I've met many stars in my time as Sasha's assistant, I'm still awestruck by many of my favorites.

Xander extends his arm. "Shall we go sit?"

I smile and hook my arm in his. "Let's do it."

A little while later, we're in fabulous seats close to the stage, and the lights are dimmed. An announcer voices the intro of the awards and then mentions the opening act. The Original Kings. Applause follows, with people whistling and stamping their feet. The curtains open, spotlights illuminate the stage, and there he is.

Axel has a brief drum solo, and then the band begins to play a song familiar to all. I clap along with everyone else in the room, and watch my brother take his place with the band, as pride fills me. I've seen him with his original and famous band, Caged Chaos, and I loved watching him then, too. But the satisfaction I see in his face now is enough to tell me this move was the right one for him.

Once I know my brother is settled, I turn my attention to Dash, who struts across the stage, singing, totally in his element. And so sexy I can't tear my gaze away.

He's removed his jacket, in which he'd looked hot enough, and now wears a fitted black tee shirt with leather jeans that mold to his perfect rear end. I bite down on my lower lip, forced to admit I'm wet just from watching him sing, aroused by the sight of his lean yet muscled body and the power of his voice.

The band segues from the fast opener to a slower tune, and the crowd goes insane as he sings the familiar award-winning refrain.

He grabs a chair someone slides out from the wings, walks to center stage, and straddles it to croon to the audience. Or so it seems. But I can see his gaze has locked on mine and he's singing directly to me.

Despite knowing that he's every woman's fantasy, *I* am the one he walked into this venue with, making a loud statement to the world. And if reality and fantasy have begun to mix in my mind, I have to admit I'm on one hell of a ride. I've stepped into an alternate universe where I am the sole focus of a rock star's attention. And I have to admit it feels really good.

The rest of the evening passes in a blur of fun and excitement. The Original Kings haven't had new music out this year. Not up for any awards, once the performance ends, they're able to relax. The guys filter into the theater area and take their seats in between live performances, until finally, a sweaty Dash joins us.

He switches seats with Xander so he can sit next to me, then grabs my hand and keeps it tight in his lap the rest of the night. I feel his hard-on against my skin.

His obvious desire is leftover adrenaline from his performance, or so I try to convince myself. It doesn't work. I know how much he desires me from the way his thigh presses close to mine and the swell of his erection pulses against my hand.

There is no way I can deny how much I want him, too.

★　★　★

Dash

I HAVE NO desire to hit the VMA after-party at Club TEN29 in Tribeca. From the moment I saw Cassidy dressed up in leather, all I've wanted is to toss her over my shoulder, find a bedroom, and fuck her all night. Good thing I had to perform, or nothing could have stopped me from acting on my desires. Nothing but Cassidy saying no, and that possibility isn't one I want to consider.

We walk out to the limousine, and I wait until we're inside before turning to talk. We have plenty of time while the limo idles, waiting for the other cars in front of us to pull out first.

"So how was your first awards show?" I want to know what she thought of my performance but don't want to ask.

I've barely gotten the words out before she's pressing me against the seat and sealing her mouth over mine. I'm stunned but don't plan to waste a moment. I kiss her, not holding back, because finally Cassidy wants me.

Her tongue darts into my mouth and rubs against mine. Sparks shoot through my system and my cock thickens, growing hard against my leather pants. She slicks her tongue across my bottom lip and pulls at it with her teeth.

I let out a groan and arch my hips, stunned when she swings one leg over my lap and straddles me, rubbing her pussy against my erection.

"Fuck," I say on a groan, worried I'm going to come in my pants. "Why am I getting so lucky?"

She doesn't hesitate. "Watching you on stage turned me on," she admits, her long lashes batting over green eyes that sparkle despite the dark limo.

"And the open bar during the show helped things along?"

She rests her hands on the shoulders of my jacket. "I admit it helped, but I already made a decision going into tonight."

I raise an eyebrow. "Oh, yeah?" My heart rate picks up speed.

She wouldn't be sitting on my lap, her legs spread, if she hadn't changed her mind about being with me. A quick fuck isn't what I want from her, but I have no idea where her mind is, if she wants to go deep like I do. And I don't just mean physically.

She pulls back, her gaze on me. "I'm aware that the times you've kissed me lately haven't been for anyone's benefit but yours. No photographers or fans. So you want me."

I roll her ponytail in my hand and tug, enjoying the low moan that escapes from her throat. "Oh, I want you, all right, but I want more than—"

She hushes me with a finger over my lips. I lick her salty skin and her eyes dilate. "You can have sex. *We* can have sex while we're pretending to be together. And when the fake relationship is over, so are we."

My gut twists in disappointment, but I'm nothing if not resourceful.

"Do we have a deal?" she asks.

I tug on her hair again, rubbing my thumb against the silken strands. "I'll take that deal," I whisper in her ear, nipping at her lobe.

And I'll use every second of that time to show her what being my woman would mean. I'll make up for how I've behaved and treat her like a queen. So when this fake relationship ends, all that remains between us will be one-hundred-percent real.

"So now you have a choice," I say, my voice rough with desire. "We can go home and do what we both want, or we can head to the after-party at Club Ten29, where I'll introduce you to celebrities, and we can watch Vivi Z. perform. Then we go home and pick up where we left off." I thrust my hips upward, and she moans at the sinful contact through our clothes.

"This isn't a fair choice," she says, laughing even as the sounds escaping her let me know what she desires.

At the husky, sexy sound, I think for sure we'll end up in my apartment bed. Because I sure as hell can't take her home to the Hamptons with Axel and the guys there.

She whispers her answer and it's my turn to groan. Because thirty minutes later, I'm walking into the Tribeca night club, Cassidy on my arm, and my very unhappy dick throbbing in my pants.

I console myself with the fact that she's given me the time I need to win her over. If not, I'll be one miserable son of a bitch when our time together comes to an end.

CHAPTER FIVE

Cassidy

I FIGURE I must be insane. I could be home in bed with my dream guy, and I've chosen to attend this loud, crowded party instead. For all I've experienced with Sasha, the VMAs are different, and I wanted to experience all that comes with being a VIP. Besides, it won't kill Dash to learn that sometimes he has to wait.

I'm not sure what's going on with his sudden kissing, attention, and desire for a relationship, nor do I know what taking it slow and not screwing up again means. I have no idea what he wants from me, but I refuse to make it as easy as a groupie he can take to bed and dispose of afterwards. Been there, done that. He can work for it, and then I'll let myself enjoy him, smarter this time, my emotions locked up tight.

No sooner do we walk in than Dash is greeted by a broad man with jet-black hair and intense blue eyes. "Kingston, it's good to see you." He shakes Dash's hand.

"You, too. I figured you'd be in town with Vivi performing tonight," Dash says.

The other man grins. "Like I'd let her go anywhere without me."

"That's right. You're her bodyguard, manager, and husband," Dash says.

"Damn right." The man obviously adores his wife and doesn't care who knows it.

I recall reading about how Vivi's husband had given up his life in New York and left the day-to-day running of his nightclub to his partners in order to travel with Vivi full-time. Now that is true love, I muse.

Dash squeezes my waist. "Cassidy Forrester, this is Landon Bennett, part owner of this club and, as you heard, Vivi's husband." He glances at the other man. "Landon, this is my *girlfriend*, Cassidy."

The word seems to slide easily off his tongue, causing an inadvertent shiver to take hold of my body.

"Cassidy was Sasha Keaton's personal assistant, and soon she'll be creative director of her new production company, K-Talent Productions," Dash goes on, pride in his voice that takes me off guard because it sounds so genuine.

I expected to be his arm candy, not someone he talks about this way.

"Great to meet you, Cassidy," Landon says with a warm smile, but I catch the initial shocked expression on his face at Dash's use of the word *girlfriend*.

"Same," I murmur. "I'm a huge Vivi Z. fan," I tell him.

"I'll try and grab her after her set so you two can meet," Landon says.

"Please do. I'd love to discuss a collab between her and the band," Dash says.

"I'll relay the message." Landon glances around and frowns. "Dammit. One of the bartenders is calling for me. I'll be sure to find you both later."

Dash hasn't released his hold on my waist. "Do you want a drink?" he asks.

"That sounds good." I'm thirsty and my mouth is parched.

"Let's see if we can get to the bar." He leans in and brushes his lips over mine, too quickly for me to react or process the action, but enough to give me a buzz even before I have more alcohol. The buzz from what little I drank at the awards has long worn off.

He leads me across the room, which takes a while. Dash is a popular guy, and we get stopped many times. No matter who he speaks to, from the biggest stars to assorted musicians and some actors, he never forgets I'm with him. He keeps his hand around my waist, publicly claiming me.

Just like with Landon, he introduces me as his girl-friend, sounding proud. He includes me in conversation and brags about my upcoming role in

Sasha, Xander, and Harrison Dare's production company, exactly like an adoring boyfriend would.

We're putting on a show, and our picture has been snapped more than a few times, ensuring we'll show up on social media, yet everything about us feels all too real.

It takes all my willpower to remember it is not. Dash isn't the kind of man who sustains a relationship, nor has he ever wanted to. I have no illusions I'll be the woman to change him. Thinking otherwise can only cause me to be even more deeply hurt. But tonight is fun and relaxed, and I know the score. I can be as flirty as I want to and enjoy his attention.

We step up to a bar with beautiful glass mirrors behind the bottles, which are lined up on shelves.

Dash edges himself up to the counter and catches the eye of a bartender.

"What can I get you, Mr. Kingston?" he asks.

"Dirty Dare Vodka, neat." He turns to me. "Cass?"

I think, then say, "I'll have a martini." Pause. Then add, "And make it dirty." I can't help but wriggle my eyebrows at him, letting him know I mean the dual meaning.

No matter how dangerous this situation is to my emotions, I've already decided I'm all in.

All but my heart.

"Here you go, dirty girl," he says, his voice low so only I can hear.

At the rumble of his voice and the awareness in his gaze, my body comes to life. He hands me the drink, his fingers deliberately touching mine. I suddenly wish I'd opted to go straight home so those hands could run over more sensitive areas, which are right now pulsing with need. I'm in for a late night, but that's okay. I'm excited for the show.

"Let's see if we can find seats," Dash says.

I nod and we wind our way around the room, finding an empty table. I've just put my purse down when I hear a familiar voice.

"Dash, great performance! I was just telling the guys watching Axel gel with you was a sight to behold. You were right in your choice." Dean slaps Dash on the back, ignoring me and the fact that I was the one to back my brother when he hadn't.

I loathe the band's manager, but damned if I'll show him he's gotten to me. Straightening my shoulders, I turn to face him.

"Agreed," Dash says. "Axel's the perfect addition."

"You looked good on the red carpet, but I still think you'd have drawn more attention with a known name on your arm." He still hasn't addressed me, and I stiffen at his insult.

So does Dash. "I thought we had this conversation. It's my life and I'll do what I want. And if you insult Cassidy one more time, even in that passive-aggressive way of yours, you'll be out on your ass, Dean." He glares at the man who has brought the band so far, but whose goals no longer align with how Dash wants to live his life.

Dean's face turns beet red, his anger obvious, but he won't make a public scene. Especially not here. "Don't forget who picked you guys up when you were nobodies," he says with a fake smile on his face.

"And you don't forget who you work for."

Shit. This could get ugly, I think. There are too many people here with camera phones and press passes. I squeeze Dash's arm in a silent reminder to calm down.

"I'm going to see another client," Dean says through clenched teeth. "I'll be in touch."

He walks away and Dash's muscles relax. He turns to face me. "Don't let him get to you."

I shrug. "He's an ass. Axel never liked him, and I'm aware he wasn't Dean's choice for your drummer. I'm just glad he has his own manager to look out for him." I think the band could use someone better, but it isn't my business.

"Dean's *choice* was a client he's been trying to turn into the next big thing, and he's never gotten over us agreeing with your assessment of what was best for the band."

I roll my eyes. "I can handle him. I just don't like him," I mutter.

His bright blue-eyed gaze fills with frustration. "He's had his own agenda for too long. I'll talk to your brother and the guys about other options."

Before we can speak further, the lights dim and strobes flash on the stage.

We take our seats beside each other, chairs facing the stage. Lights flash and loud applause surrounds us as Vivi strides onto the stage.

Dash wraps one arm around me and slides his other hand over my bare thigh, drumming a beat with those tempting fingers on my skin.

I immediately squirm, desire beginning to pulse inside me to the beat of the music. I could grab his wrist to stop him but why? It's dark and I want his touch. He inches his fingers higher, the forbidden movement hidden by both the lack of lighting and the table above.

Dash takes advantage, his thumb making long strokes across my skin until he reaches the edge of my shorts. He teases me, dipping his finger beneath the hem, but the leather is tight, and he can't move up far enough to give me any kind of relief. He leans in close, his breath warm on my cheek. "Do you have any idea what I want to do to you?"

He lifts his hand off my thigh, and taking me off

guard, he sweeps that teasing finger across my sex, pressing against the leather and making sure he pushes against my clit. "And I will, the minute I get you alone."

He releases the pressure and I want to cry in frustration. No doubt that was his intent. As he clasps my hand in his, I have no choice but to watch and listen to Vivi, the talented artist, sing and perform for the admiring crowd. It isn't easy to concentrate, not with the wetness in my skimpy underwear and the empty pulsing in my core. Meanwhile, jaw tight, looking equally antsy, Dash keeps his gaze on the stage.

When the set ends and the lights brighten the room, Sasha and Xander find us and settle into empty seats.

While the brothers chat, Sasha leans into me. "How's it going?" she asks.

"I'm having a great time," I murmur.

"Is something wrong?" Sasha wrinkles her nose as she studies me. "Need a ladies' trip to the restroom?" My friend knows me too well.

But I don't need girl talk to make my decision about tonight, so I shake my head. Besides, no way do I want to walk around more than I have to. The tight pants will brush against my sensitive areas and make things worse. "I'm okay. Dash has just been very…"

"Touchy?" Sasha asks, glancing down at Dash's

hand still wrapped around mine.

"Shh." But I feel the blush stealing across my cheeks. I need a change of subject. "You did a wonderful job presenting the award," I tell my friend.

Sasha sweeps her long blond hair to the side and smiles. "Thank you. I was glad when it was over. These award ceremonies can feel endless. So much waiting. So where are you staying tonight? Xander wants to go back to his apartment uptown, and Axel said he'd take care of Bella. Xander gave him a key to the house so he could walk and feed her."

"Aww. That's sweet. My brother's a softy sometimes. He loves animals." I bite the inside of my cheek. "I'm not sure what our plans are. I didn't intend to stay in the city, but it *is* a long ride back."

I glance around, not wanting to give Sasha an opportunity to ask questions about my curious relationship with Dash.

During my perusal, I catch sight of an uber-famous couple. "Oh, look! Megan Fox and Machine Gun Kelly!" I whisper, doing my best not to squeal and gesture like the fangirl I am.

Sasha chuckles and proceeds to subtly nod and point out different actors and musicians and whisper stories about each.

"Well, look who's here. My new business partners." Harrison Dare grabs a chair from another table and settles his large body into the seat. He grins at Sasha and Xander, saying his hellos before turning to me and Dash.

"What are you doing here?" Dash asks. "I thought you were filming a movie?"

"My cousin is part-owner of this bar," he says. "I wouldn't miss him hosting such a huge event. Even if Jason has been too busy to sit down for five minutes and catch up." He grins and glances at me. We've met before, when he was on set with Sasha during one of the period pieces they'd starred in together.

"You're looking beautiful tonight." Harrison appraises me with a warm glint in his indigo eyes.

A rumble sounds from deep in Dash's throat, loud despite the crowd and the background music, and he settles his hand around the back of my neck, staking his claim.

I would shoot him an annoyed look if I could turn to meet his gaze, but he has me locked in place beside him.

"Thank you, Harrison. How are you?" I ask the other man. After my stint as a personal assistant for the band, members of whom I've seen wandering around tonight, I'll be working closely with all three of the partners at K-Talent Productions, and I'm not about to be rude to Harrison.

"All is good here, thanks," he says. "Vodka?" He

gestures to my martini and Dash's drink with a know-ing grin.

I nod. "Only the best," I say, letting him know it's his family's brand they we're drinking.

His answering smile is sexy, made more so thanks to one side tooth that overlaps another. Just short of perfection, Harrison Dare is a movie star with a face made for the big screen, eyes a unique color and his black hair just begging for a woman to run her fingers through the longer strands.

And if I wasn't so hooked on a suddenly posses-sive rock star, I might be tempted to flirt. What red-blooded woman wouldn't want this man's attention? But my panties are damp from Dash's touch and my body primed from all his attention.

Somehow I'm going to have to make good on my self-imposed promise to take advantage of what the man offers and not get my heart hurt in the process.

Harrison turns to Dash. "Great performance to-night," he says, extending his hand.

"Thanks." The begrudging sound nearly makes me choke. Does he really think Harrison is hitting on me? Or that I'm at all interested?

I imagine the two men nearly break each other's fingers during their shake.

Apparently Sasha has been watching and shoots me an amused grin.

I roll my eyes. "Men," I mouth to my friend and receive a nod in return.

Soon, Sasha, Xander, and Harrison begin talking shop, and Dash leans over. "I'm ready to get the hell out of here. How about you?"

I swallow hard. "Yes."

Relief crosses his handsome face. "My apartment is closer."

"I didn't bring a change of clothes."

He grins. "You won't be needing any. Besides, Chloe left sweats and some things there you can borrow."

"Sounds like you've got this all figured out."

He runs a finger down my cheek. "When it comes to you? Not even close."

Dash

THE RIDE BACK to my apartment isn't long, but I'm not sure I can wait to get my hands on Cassidy. She looks so fucking gorgeous on my arm, making me proud to show her off to everyone I know. Even calling her my girlfriend wasn't difficult, and for a man who's avoided relationships, that's saying something huge.

Just looking at her has me sporting wood. I would take her to the bathroom and fuck her here and now if I didn't respect her so damned much and want to make a better impression than the one I've already left her with. Then again, my bed is probably a better option. I can take my time and get to know every part of her luscious body.

Still, there's no reason I can't get this started now. We know from our ride here that the driver can't see or hear us unless the partition comes down. We have all the privacy we need.

As I did during Vivi's set, I place my hand on Cassidy's knee and begin to slowly trail my fingers up her bare skin. I already know her tight shorts will hinder my efforts, but that's okay. There is time to get where I want. We have all night.

Leaning toward her, I wind my fingers around her long ponytail, feeling the silky softness while at the same time cupping her cheek. "I've been waiting hours to get you all to myself."

Those sparkling eyes twinkle as I speak. "What are you going to do now that you have me?"

I lick her glossed lips once. Twice. The third time, I yank on her hair at the same time I seal my mouth over hers. Like we've been let off leash, we devour each other, lips clashing, tongues tangling, teeth nipping as I experience the hottest kiss of my life.

I've never wanted anyone as badly as I do Cassidy, and apparently she feels the same way. Needing to know for sure, I cup her sex in my hands, feeling her heat through the material.

I pull back, breaking the kiss. "Are you wet for me?" I ask, my gruff voice barely recognizable even to myself.

"Why don't you find out for yourself?" she asks.

This is the woman I remember from our night together. The uninhibited female who needs me as much as I do her and isn't afraid to tease or to take what she wants.

I doubt she's forgiven me, but it's clear she's decided to give in to our desire. Whatever her reasons, any chance to get closer to her, I'll take it.

I unhook the clasps of her jacket, revealing a thin black stretch camisole that hugs her skin and shows off her full breasts. Easily, I lift the hem of her top and slide my fingers beneath the elastic waistband of her shorts, inching downward until I encounter her hot, wet warmth.

"Fuck." I press my forehead to hers, trying to catch my breath as I strum her nearly bare sex.

"Oh God, Dash, harder." Her hips buck upward, seeking a firmer, deeper connection.

One I want to give her.

I have every intention of pushing the shorts

around her thighs and baring her sweet pussy so I can stroke her until she comes. Then I'll lower my head and give myself a long, leisurely taste, sucking her juices. At the thought, my cock threatens to explode from the confines of my pants.

Given the size of this limo, I know I have plenty of room to get a taste of her before we get back to my apartment.

I hook my hands into her elastic waistband and pull her shorts down, panties along with them, easing them both to her feet and pulling them off. I pick up the tiny scrap of lace and shove it into my jacket pocket before turning my attention back to her again.

Need shimmers in her gaze, and her teeth bite into her plump bottom lip in anticipation as she watches me. I drop to my knees, and she parts her legs, welcoming me.

My cock wants more than I plan to take right now, so I grip myself hard through the leather, trying to control my need. I want to take care of her first. Without wasting a moment, I grasp her thighs and slide my tongue over her sensitive folds. I shut my eyes, savoring my first taste.

She is everything I remember and more. I hum in approval, and she arches up, moaning as I begin my assault. I lick and suck, pulling her lips into my mouth, then releasing her flesh.

I slide two fingers into her sex. "Is this good?" I ask, pumping in and out, finding the soft spot inside her that has her writhing against the seat.

She raises one arm above her head, her hand hitting the window. The other hand fists in my hair and pulls as I rub inside her.

"Oh, oh, yes. Yes." Her hips move up and down in time to my movements.

The noises coming out of her have me hard as granite. Ignoring it is hell but I can take it. She is so close and that's what I want. I've spent so much time thinking about making her come again. Focusing on her pleasure instead of my own.

I lick her again, giving my attention to her clit, caressing the tiny bud with my tongue before taking it between my lips and sucking hard. She spreads her legs, providing me even better access, and I brace my hand over her belly so she can't thrash off the seat. She's ready and I nip at her clit, pushing her to the edge, then over it, and sucking and soothing until she collapses.

While she pulls in deep breaths, I wipe my hand across my mouth and return to my seat. I lean over and kiss her. She kisses me back, shocking me when she welcomes her taste on my lips and sealing, at least in my mind, our relationship.

I am deep in it and not protesting that fact. At least

not to myself. Now I just have to convince her.

As if on cue, the limo pulls to the side of the street and comes to a stop. We've reached my apartment. I know the driver will idle the vehicle until I rap on the partition, letting him know that we're ready to get out.

I glance at the woman splayed against the seat. Her ponytail hangs in disarray and the sexy strands fall around her face. Her lips are puffy from my kisses and her cheeks flushed with arousal. She's never looked more beautiful.

I run my knuckles down her cheek. "Time to take this upstairs." Reaching over, I lift her shorts for her to put on.

"Where are my panties?" she asks, looking around.

"You're not getting those back." I pat my pocket and treat her to a shameless grin.

Though she rolls her eyes, an adorable flush stains her cheeks before she focuses on wriggling her shorts back into place.

I re-hook her jacket, making sure she's covered in case we run into someone in the lobby. The doorman won't say a word. He's seen plenty in his time on the job. Not from me. I never bring groupies home to my sanctuary. Which means I've never brought any woman to my place before.

It seems fitting that Cassidy be the first. "Ready?" I ask her.

She glances at me through heavy-lidded eyes and nods.

I rap on the partition.

A few seconds later, the driver opens the door and extends his hand. Cassidy slides out first, and I notice she doesn't meet the man's gaze. I climb out and thank the driver, who is well paid for his discretion, not to mention the NDA every one of the company employees signs. Taking her hand, I lead her inside, through the lobby, and into the elevator.

The doors close. I don't know who moves first, but suddenly she's in my arms, her hand around my neck and my mouth on hers. I put everything I need into that kiss, all that I've held back in the limousine while concentrating on her.

The elevator dings and comes to a stop, the doors opening. Good thing the penthouse gives me the entire floor to myself. We step directly into my apartment and we kick off our shoes.

Cassidy walks to the large windows making up the far back wall, and I follow, the darkness of the city below surrounding us. While I watch, she works the hooks on the leather jacket, letting the garment fall to the floor. Lifting the edge of her camisole, she pulls it over her head and flings it … somewhere. A push-up bra holds up those gorgeous breasts, and she keeps it on as she bends down and slides off the shorts, leaving her pussy bare. Only then does she straighten, reach behind her, unclasp her bra, and let it fall to the floor.

"Jesus, you're gorgeous." And smart, witty, not to mention able to handle anything life throws at her. Including me.

Our first time in the hotel room was fast and frenzied, with her needing comfort and to forget her friend being hurt and the stalker who'd terrorized them. I had been my asshole self. Meaning, I was in it for gratification and pleasure. Instead I've found the most incredible woman, who I have no doubt now is meant for me and who deserves more.

"Thank you," she murmurs. "Now it's your turn." She steps toward me and shrugs my jacket off my shoulders.

I catch a whiff of the exotic scent that is a part of her and groan, immediately working on removing my pants while she pulls my tee shirt up and I help her get it over my head.

The second I'm naked, I draw her soft body against mine, feeling her heat as it seeps into my skin. I kiss her, softer than in the limo, my hands wandering over her curves and velvety flesh.

"One day I'm going to fuck you in front of this window with the entire city as the backdrop."

"No promises," she says, kissing my lips in an obvious attempt to shut him up.

She doesn't believe me, and I don't blame her, accepting the pain in my gut as my due. All I can do is stay the course and convince her.

"Fine." I swallow back an argument. "I want you in the one place no woman's ever been." I bend and hook a hand beneath her knees, sweeping her into my arms.

"What?" She wraps her arms around my neck to steady herself, but I see the disbelief in her eyes.

"I didn't say I was a saint." There've been many females in my life. Too many to remember. "I said no woman's ever been in my bed." I walk through the darkened apartment to the master bedroom and settle her on top of the king mattress. "Until you."

"I don't think—"

That is the problem. I'm giving her too much time to use that smart brain of hers, and the more she adds up, the less she believes me. So I kiss her until she can't agonize over every word I say, my past, or the future. I kiss her until she lays back on the bed, and I follow her down, my body covering hers, my cock pressing hard into her belly.

I'm doing enough thinking for both of us. I don't want tonight to be a fling with a rock star. Not for her. I've been working hard to prove that I'm no longer the cavalier womanizer I once was, and I haven't had nearly enough time to show her anything about me that is real. That will change starting tomorrow morning. We'll talk. I'll open up, as difficult as the thought is. And hopefully she'll see the man beneath the façade.

Tonight I need to be inside her. For as long and for as many times as she'll let me. Taking me by surprise, she reaches between us, wrapping her hand around my cock, sending darts of pleasure through my system. My dick is hard. Pre-come pools on the head, and she swipes her thumb over the tip.

I groan at her playful touch, but my balls ache and I need her *now*. "I have to get a condom." I roll off her and pull open the drawer where I keep a box, and grab a packet.

But when I return to her, she's sitting up, legs drawn up to her chest, watching me warily.

I sigh, knowing I've just put another barrier between us. "I have them so I can keep one in my wallet. I won't use a random one that some chick provides," I mutter.

"Lovely." Her expression has shut down.

"Cassidy, I didn't lie to you about no other woman being in this bed. And I'm going to tell you again, something you don't want to believe, but it's the God's honest truth."

She appears ready to bolt, so I blurt it out. "I haven't slept with anyone else since that night with you."

★ ★ ★

Cassidy

DAMN, THIS MAN has my mind going in too many directions, confusing me and making me wonder what I can believe. Then again, does it matter? I've already committed to being with Dash, which means he has no reason to lie. I decide to trust him … to a point.

"Are we good?" he asks.

He kneels beside me, his tanned, muscled body a heady temptation, his expression sincere and contrite. Not to mention the way he looks at me, his long hair falling over his forehead, his eyes, the desire in them obvious. Why am I wasting time being hurt about his past when we can be together now?

"We're fine," I tell him. "You can't change your past and I shouldn't worry about it."

To prove my point, I reach out and grasp his semi-hard cock in my hands. I've ruined the mood but that won't be for long. I slide my hand up and down, rubbing my thumb over the tip until his hips jerk upward and he lets out a rumbling groan. That's better.

I continue to stroke him, and he leans over, licking my nipple, pulling it into his mouth, and flicking it with his tongue. Desire hits me and I moan, my sex growing wet, ribbons of need winding through me, and I grip his cock harder in my hand.

"Damn, Cass, you need to stop before I come."

"Then hurry," I whisper.

He grabs the condom from the bed, rips the packet open, and rolls it down his shaft. Shifting over me, he kissed me, a slow, languid stroking of his lips against mine that leaves me shaking with need. As he slips his tongue into my mouth, he settles himself at my entrance, and raising his hips, he pushes himself in.

We groan in unison, coming up for air because he fits so perfectly. Clenching his jaw, he works himself deep but I need more. I part my legs and bend my knees so I can accept all of him.

"You feel so good around my cock," he says, nipping at my ear.

I squeeze my inner walls, and he throbs inside me, causing me to drop my head back against the pillow. He dips his head and licks my bare neck, then sucks on my flesh, and my sex pulses in answering need. Then he begins to move, thrusting in and out, my body accepting him as if we were made for each other.

His hands are braced beside my head, and he shifts his hips so each plunge hits me in just the right spot. "Yes," I moan, scraping my nails against his back. "More, Dash, please. I need you." The words are torn from me along with a sound I've never made before.

He reaches between us and circles my clit until pleasure flows through me even more. I clench him tighter and sensual ripples begin to torment me. I raise my hips and he thrusts harder, taking me up and over.

I fly and cry out as I come. He lets go and I feel him surrender, taking me deeper into the never-ending pleasure he's created. I can't think, can't do anything but feel. Without the ability to think, a little voice in the back of my head tells me I'm floating in a very good, very safe space, and I give up the fight.

CHAPTER SIX

Cassidy

I WAKE FROM a deep sleep, a heavy arm wrapped around my waist and a familiar masculine hand cupping my bare breast. In that hazy space between unconsciousness and wakefulness, I snuggle into the warm body spooning me in an attempt to stay in this dreamlike state a little while longer. Before reality and the light of day bring my worries and fears to life.

Dash wraps himself more thoroughly around me, which causes me to drop my head back against him and sigh. *This could become my favorite way to be woken up,* and on that thought, the blanket of peace evaporates, leaving my rapidly beating heart in its wake.

"No. Don't go into panic mode." He presses his lips against my shoulder and kisses me. "Just relax and go with it," he says, licking my skin and nuzzling where my jaw meets my neck.

Liquid pools between my thighs, and I can't help but do as he says, relaxing into *us.* Without missing a beat, I reach behind me to thread my hand into his hair and pull him closer. I turn my head as much as I can to bring him in for a kiss.

Dash groans into my mouth. "God, I want you."

He shifts away and opens the drawer. The tear of the condom wrapper follows before he wraps himself around me once more. "Lift your leg."

I do as he commands, and with some maneuvering, he slides into me from behind. I hold back a whimper as he enters me, his thickness filling me until I feel like a part of him.

Without waiting, he begins to move, our joining more of a slow rocking than a hard pounding. This is intense and emotional for reasons I can't begin to fathom. Nor do I want to. I push that sense of belonging away and close my eyes, focusing on our physical connection until the movement of his hips and the glide of his cock inside me are all I can feel.

"Fuck," he mutters, his tone somewhere between a prayer and a curse.

I don't care which it is, as long as he doesn't stop.

But he pulls out, and before I can protest, he rolls me onto my back and climbs between my thighs, his alert gaze intent on mine.

He leans forward, rubbing his erection against my sex, and a wave of pleasure beckons and drifts away, leaving me empty.

"Do you like being woken up this way?" he asks as he slides against me again, teasing me.

"I thought I was dreaming."

"No dream, baby." He rubs his length over my clit, and a shudder ripples through me. "But you didn't tell me if you liked it."

Too much, I think, but I'm not about to admit my insecurities. "It's the best wake-up call I've ever had."

He gives me that sexy rock star grin. "I'm happy to give you many more," he says, arching his hips and pushing deep again.

To my frustration, he stills inside me, as if savoring the moment. *Silly girl.* Men don't react that way. Especially a man like Dash Kingston. Yet another reason to ignore the promise of more I know he won't keep and remain focused on the here and now.

"No more teasing." I lift my body off the mattress, pulling him deeper inside me, squeezing her inner walls tight.

"There's the dirty girl who ordered that drink last night." Desire darkens his gaze and a bead of sweat forms on his forehead.

Dammit. Even his gruff voice is a turn-on.

He slides out and pushes back, filling me completely, so much so that when he eases back, the emptiness is real. But then he begins to move in earnest, pounding into me and taking me on the ride of my life.

"I'm not going to last long, though," he tells me,

our slow, emotional rocking of earlier now a frenzied needy thing.

Both ways are somehow reaching the heart I've tried to protect, and with each thrust, I fall for him a little more. He slides a hand between us and rubs my clit. He circles his thumb twice before I tighten around him, the glorious waves beginning to take me over.

I've never been so responsive to a man before, and last time I thought it was just Dash's experience that makes him so good. Now I consider that it's the two of us together. An even more dangerous thought.

He lifts his hand, brings his thumb to his mouth, and quickly sucks it in before returning to her clit. One quick slide and I'm coming, crying out and circling my hips to grind against him and trigger his release.

He pumps in and out quickly before he stills, breathing against that sweet spot where my shoulder meets my neck, until he collapses against me.

I thread my hands through his hair, breathing hard along with him. A few perfect seconds pass until he slips out of me. Before rolling off the bed, he pulls me in for another kiss.

He heads for the bathroom. I need one, too, and push myself up to a sitting position before stretching, the covers dropping below my breasts.

"Do not tempt me," he says on a low growl, returning to the side of the bed. He stares, his gaze hot on my bare upper body. I glance at his cock, which has grown hard and erect again. For me.

The sight pleases me. Knowing I can keep arousing Dash the rock star is a powerful thing for a regular girl like me. Too bad the parts of him I like go deeper than the man I've seen owning the stage.

Dash, the man who loves his siblings, who makes sure I'm comfortable among celebrities, who brags about my job to people who couldn't care less, and who wasn't self-centered in the least, is hard to resist.

I need to pull myself together, and another round of sex won't do it. My stomach rumbles loudly, making it easier. "I'm starving," I say, grasping my belly and refusing to be embarrassed.

"We worked up an appetite." He treats me to a wink. "How about we order in breakfast?"

"I love delivery in Manhattan," I say. "The city has so many more choices."

He kisses me twice quickly. "I'm going to order, then I'll take a quick shower so I'm around to get the door. You can take your time after me."

Giving orders. What else is new? With a groan, I flop against the pillows, wondering when I lost control of my life.

A LITTLE WHILE later, I'm clean and well fed and sitting across from Dash at the kitchen table near a window overlooking the city, wearing one of his large band tee shirts and nothing underneath.

He has on a pair of track pants and no shirt, his tanned skin and lean muscles tempting me as I sit beside him. Sexy scruff covers the lower half of his face, and because of that facial hair, I have stubble burn on my upper thighs. I do my best not to squirm at the memory.

We've eaten our omelets and bacon and are now drinking our coffee.

I pick up my mug and take a sip. "I looked over the band's schedule, and the next two weeks are quiet."

He nods. "That's good. I'm going to need you to set up a meet and greet at the Hamptons Rehab Center. The timing is perfect."

I raise an eyebrow, surprised. "Of course. Do you want me to give the information to Naomi?" I ask of the band's publicist.

"No. Absolutely not." The rough sound of his voice combined with the determined note in it tells me all I need to know.

"Under the radar it is."

His shoulders ease and he leans back in his seat. "It's something I do for myself and an old friend. I don't want any kind of accolades or media attention."

"Okay," I say quietly, sensing how important this is to him. "I love that you do this. I'm sure it gives people who are struggling a boost they need."

I glance down. "I hope so."

Because the time is right, I decide to open up to him. "My parents were killed by someone driving while impaired by drugs. Someone who, it turns out, had been refusing rehab when his family asked, then begged him to go."

He visibly stiffens and I twist my hands in my lap. I never like talking about their deaths but I…trust him with personal, painful information.

"Is he in jail?" Dash asks.

I shake my head. "He died that night, too."

"I'm sorry," he says in a gruff voice.

I meet his gaze and give him a smile. "Me, too." Clearing my throat, I sense a subject change is in order. "Anything else you want me to line up?"

He seems to relax again. "No. I'll be going into the studio with the guys to do some collaboration, see what we can come up with." Excitement glitters in his eyes at the prospect.

"Have you been writing? I know Axel comes up with his own lyrics, too."

He nods. "I might even have been inspired by a certain woman who brings unexpected light to my life." His sexy grin lights me up inside.

I shake my head again, refusing to believe he's serious. "Come on. You already got me into bed. No need to try and charm me now," I say, still thinking he's joking.

He tightens up and I feel him withdraw. "Is that what you think I'm doing? Trying to charm you and not telling you the truth?" Hurt sounds in his voice, making me feel small.

I hate that my insecurities have led me to belittle what he said. "You really wrote songs about me?" I whisper.

"You're damn right I did." Reaching out, he pulls me off his chair and onto his lap, taking me by surprise. "I know you don't trust me, and I've given you good reason, but I hope you'll try and keep an open mind from here on in."

I've already trusted him, I think, as I loop my arms around his neck and touch my forehead to his. "I'll try harder," I promise him.

A slow smile crosses his face, and he presses his mouth against mine. Tasting coffee on his lips, I moan and touch my tongue to his. The kiss doesn't last long because the ring of his phone interrupts us, sounding from its place on the table.

He groans and glances at his cell. "Sorry. Give me a minute."

He reaches over and picks up his phone, answering the call. "Hey, Mom."

I open my eyes wide and try to squirm off his lap, but his strong arm holds her tight. Thanks to my movement, I feel him harden beneath my thighs, and arousal suddenly pulses through me as well.

As if nothing is wrong, he focuses on his call. "Thanks," he says to his mom. "I'm glad you loved the show on television. The guys and I had a great time performing."

Once again I attempt an escape, but he clasps a hand on my upper thigh, and I swallow a squeak of both surprise and objection.

"But it's your mother," I mouth, shaking my head.

He ignores me, keeping me in place, something his erection obviously enjoys. "Yes, I know the family barbeque is this Sunday at my place. It's not a problem."

I am well aware of the Kingston family get-togethers, big events that include friends as well as the relatives at least once a month. I've been invited, too, in the past, courtesy of Sasha.

"Oh, you saw the red carpet?" He winks at me and grins. "Yes, I'm with Cassidy now. Yep. Official girlfriend."

I poke him in the chest, and he grabs my finger, still grinning.

He shouldn't be lying to his mother. This is a fake arrangement to help his social media presence settle down so he can focus on his music. Now that the world knows about us, he'll have a couple of quiet weeks in the Hamptons, and the potential-baby-daddy drama should blow over. As it is, mentions are slowing down to a trickle. If the guys stay out of bars and trouble and lay low for a while, my job will be done. I ignore the cramping in my stomach at the thought of losing *this*, and I hold his arm tighter against me.

He chuckles at something his mother says. "We were taking things slow, that's why you didn't know about it." He listens then says, "Of course she'll be there on Sunday."

I close my eyes and sigh.

"Yep. I will. Love you, too, Mom. Bye." He disconnects the call and puts his phone on the table.

Then he glances at me, still holding me on his lap with his arm, and smiles, the genuine Dash smile I adore.

"Stop trying to soften me up," I mutter. "You shouldn't be lying to your mom."

He raises an eyebrow. "Is telling her what I believe to be true lying? We're together."

"Officially?"

"As far as the world … and I am concerned, we are." His expression grows serious. "Stop worrying."

He presses a kiss to my lips. "You'll be at the barbeque?" he asks.

I feel the lift of my lips into a smile. "You told Melly I'd be there. How can I not show up?" I ask.

"Good. Mom will be happy."

Everyone loves Melly Kingston. How can you not appreciate a woman who takes in her dead husband's pregnant, adult child from an affair and easily makes her and her baby part of the family? Melly has never blamed Aurora for her husband's behavior, and since the young woman grew up in foster care thanks to neglectful parents, it makes Melly's acceptance all the more sweet.

Dash's mother has always treated me well, too. I won't mislead her … and Dash has a point. It isn't a lie. We *are* together—for now. And that's all I need to remember.

I hop off his lap, and because I've taken him off guard, he lets me go and I settle back into my seat.

He shoots me a knowing gaze but doesn't say anything about my escaping.

"You enjoy my family, right?" Dash asks.

I nod. I've always envied him his big family with a lot of siblings and closeness. All I have is my brother, and sometimes I get lonely. During the last four years, I've had Sasha in my life. We're like sisters, and we spent holidays together if Axel wasn't in town, but now Sasha has Xander. And though they'd never not include me, I don't want to be a third wheel.

"Where'd you go?" Dash asks, breaking into my thoughts.

I glance up. "I was just thinking how lucky you guys are to have such a big family. I love my brother but holidays can get lonely." I set my jaw, wondering what made me confide in him that way. If I'm going to protect myself, I can't be too vulnerable with him.

His expression softens. "You're always welcome at any family gathering we have. Sasha wouldn't have it any other way and neither would I."

"I appreciate you saying that." Especially since there will be times Dash and I will have to be in the same room for an event once whatever *this* is between us ends. Not that I'm bringing that up now and upsetting the balance we've found.

"My siblings are great but my family situation wasn't always the best." Dash picks up his coffee and takes a long sip.

I'm not looking at his lips and remembering how they feel on mine. *I'm really not,* I think, waiting for him to tell me more.

"My father didn't understand me, and trust me when I tell you, sometimes I thought no father would have been preferable to Kenneth Kingston's disapproval."

I frown at that, realizing that it's his turn to open up to me, and I want to know everything about him. I don't know much regarding the family's background beyond the fact that his sister, Aurora, is new to the clan, having been tracked down by Linc this year after their father passed away. Sasha protects Xander's past and secrets, and I have always respected their relationship. It doesn't affect me and so I haven't asked.

"Your father didn't recognize your talent?" I ask him.

Dash shakes his head. "Wasn't interested, either. He really was an absent father unless we embarrassed him or he had to clean up a mess," he mutters.

"What do you mean? What kind of mess?" I ask.

"I'll explain … one day. I just don't want to ruin our weekend with shitty stories about the past."

I narrow my gaze. "Okay, but I'm here if you ever want to open up."

He dips his head. "I know. And it's probably the only time I owe my father for helping me out. Hell," he says, running a hand through his hair, "I'm not even sure he did the right thing back then."

He has me curious, but it's also evident he isn't ready to talk about it, and I won't pressure him.

"And after my father died, we found out that he'd been a serial cheater, which explains why he was never around. But when he was? He bitched about the music

I played, the friends I hung out with, the time I spent trying to create a band, and he belittled my dreams. So no. He didn't recognize my talent."

I wince. At least our grandmother fostered Axel's music abilities. "I'm sorry."

"It's fine." He waves a hand as if blowing it off. "I had Mom and my siblings. It all worked out."

Somehow I doubt that. Parental disapproval leaves lingering internal scars, and I touch his hand, meaning to comfort him.

"Don't worry about me. I made out fine in the end, right?" he asks lightly.

I frown at his too-easy answer. "Dash the rock star made out fine. How about Dash the man?"

A hint of vulnerability shows in his expression, something I sense he doesn't often reveal and something else we have in common. "Thanks to the band, I got out of the house more often than not. I had a goal and I worked toward it."

"And you accomplished everything you dreamed of. Whether or not your father was proud doesn't matter." I rise, intending to clean up our coffee, which has grown cold.

Unable to help myself, I lean over and touch my forehead to his. "Your mom, your brothers, and your sisters are proud." I swallow hard before admitting, "*I'm* proud."

His hands grasp my hips and he rises to his feet. "You have no idea what that means to me."

Our gazes meet and hold. With his help, I jump up and wrap my legs around his waist. Holding me against him, he walks us to the bedroom, lays me down on the mattress, and before I know it, he's sheathed himself and thrust deep. Once he's inside me, I can only focus on him, as again he wipes away my insecurities and makes promises with his body I pray he can keep.

Dash

LATER IN THE day, I have the band's on-call car service send someone to pick us up in the city. On the trip home, Cassidy dozes, her head falling against my shoulder, and I ease her into a more comfortable position, one arm wrapped around her.

During the silent trip, I marvel at her strength and ability to make it through the red carpet and the party afterward. Forgetting how she looked, which had me hard all night, she'd impressed me with her ability to charm everyone we met. I'd introduced her as more than arm candy, and my friends, from musicians to actors, were warm, accepting, and definitely approving. I was proud to have her by my side.

Waking up with my arms around her had been a first. Usually I fuck and get the hell out of there, doing my best to make a statement about what the often nameless woman meant to me. With Cassidy, I was relaxed, happy, and fuck if I hadn't wanted to slide into her without a condom. Only my recent scare and common sense had me reaching for protection before gliding into her wet heat.

It was the most intimate I've ever been with a female, and with Cass, I want to repeat that kind of closeness again and again. Does it scare me? Hell yes. It isn't like it's easy to go from playboy to wanting a relationship without shocking moments along the way. But I am in it and not pulling back. I just hope when she finds out about my past, she doesn't view me differently, especially given how her parents died.

When the driver reaches her house, I walk her to the door, leaving her with a kiss I hope she'll remember, before heading to my place.

As always, when I pull up to my beach house, I say a prayer of gratitude for the life I have. Too many people in my industry and life in general end up on drugs, usually mixed with alcohol, and it often doesn't end well.

I'm lucky my wake-up call came early and that I'd heeded it. Substance abuse is a part of the lifestyle but not for me, and the guys know drugs are taboo in my house. I'd throw them out of the band if they brought that shit into my home.

Talking to Cassidy about my family was easy. Revealing the most painful part of my life was not. I intend to get to a place with her where I can share that pain. If I'd wanted to tell her earlier, her revelation about the driver on drugs who killed her parents gave me pause.

At some point before or after we do the meet and greet at the rehab center, I'll have to open up to her. Besides my family, nobody else knows about that time in my life. I understand what a big deal it is that I want Cassidy to know and forgive me the way I'm still working on forgiving myself.

I walk into the house, and the first thing I notice is the quiet. Unusual when you live with three other guys. I head to the sliding glass doors that lead to the pool, but no one is there, so I walk into the kitchen to find Axel sitting with a half-finished bottle of beer.

From the dark look on his face, the man has been waiting for me to get home.

I should have been prepared for this and ready to explain, but I've been so wrapped up in Cassidy, I forgot about her brother. My new bandmate.

"I take it you slept in the city," Axel says before I can speak.

I pull out a chair and join him. "It was a long ride

back. I figured I'd stay at my apartment."

Axel nods, rubbing his thumb along the paper on the bottle. "You mean *we*, don't you? You and Cass? Because my sister wasn't home today and she didn't answer her cell."

I decide to tread cautiously and remember that I, too, have sisters I love and feel protective over. I open my mouth but Axel cuts me off.

"And don't tell me you two were just acting like you're in a relationship … unless she slept in the guest room?" As Axel pins me with green eyes similar to Cassidy's, I make a decision then and there not to lie.

Cassidy might be pissed, but if I lay it out for her brother, won't it help convince her of my sincerity? Not to mention, I can't afford to piss off the new guy in the band and fuck up the future for everyone.

I will, however, for Cassidy's sake, tiptoe around how I explain. "She wasn't in the guest room, but I am not using your sister," I say at the same time Axel shoves his chair back and rises, fists clenched at his sides.

I nod to the chair. "Sit down and let's discuss this like rational human beings."

A second passes, then two. Finally, jaw set, Axel repositions the chair and sits down. "My sister acts like nothing hurts her but that's bullshit. She just told herself she and that douchebag Adam had drifted apart. That his breaking up with her by text was no big deal. But she was hurt. Badly. Since our parents died, she stuffs her emotions way down and pretends she's fine."

I wince. "I didn't know the asshole did that to her." Looks like Cassidy has some revealing of her own to do, I think.

"He did. Only reason I didn't go after him was because I know she's better off." Axel meets my gaze. "As for you—" He begins to tick off points on his fingers. "Your reputation with women precedes you. You're barely off a baby scare with a groupie. And you did agree to *pretend* to be in a relationship with my sister."

"All true," I admit. "But the only reason I agreed with Naomi's idea was because I wanted a chance with Cassidy. She wouldn't let me near her otherwise."

"Why not?"

His question tells me what I already assumed. Cassidy hasn't told her brother about our first night together.

Resigned, I meet Axel's stormy gaze. "I fucked up with her once already, and before you haul off and hit me, if your sister wanted you to know anything about our relationship, she'd have told you."

The other man's scowl is deep, and he's muscular enough to make it a fair fight. I wait for him to blow, but so far Axel sits in tense silence.

So I take advantage and go on. "I've opened up to you the little I have because I respect you and I want the band to work with you in it." I lean one elbow on the granite tabletop. "But Cassidy is an adult. I've told you I'm not using her, and I'll take it one step further and admit that I'm trying to build something real. So I'm asking you to back off and let us figure it out for ourselves."

I wait a few beats, letting Axel process the situation before holding out a hand, hoping we've come to an understanding. That Axel will accept and call a truce.

Enough time passes that I wonder if I've lost another drummer. Finally, Axel extends his arm and shakes my hand, squeezing hard when he speaks. "Hurt her and I won't give a shit about the band. You'll pay."

"Fair enough." I would feel the same about Chloe or Aurora. Relieved, I expel a long breath.

Both men stand.

"Where are the guys?" I ask.

"They both left the after-party with some chicks and haven't been home." Axel picks up the beer bottle and pours what must be flat by now into the sink.

"What about you?" I ask.

He lifts a shoulder. "Not in the mood, I guess." He pauses and glances at me. "You're feeling it, aren't you? The groupies and shit? It's getting old."

"You wouldn't think twenty-eight is old but yeah, I do. It's been too many years of the same old." I shake my head. "That baby scare shook me up. Ending up parenting with someone I don't know and barely remember?" I shudder at the reminder of what I've escaped. "Then I look at Xander and Sasha and my sister and Beck, and I want more."

That more being Cassidy. A woman who thinks for herself, is smart and driven. She doesn't take my shit, and I don't want to give her any. She is a warm, caring person who was there for her best friend during a scary time and hadn't run at the first sign of danger. I want her to turn that caring part of her nature on me, without being afraid I'll hurt her. And I want to give her the security she deserves and take away the loneliness she doesn't.

Axel listens and nods. "Same, man. Same." He slaps me on the back and walks out of the kitchen.

Staring after him, I realized I've just received Axel's permission. I would have continued my pursuit of Cassidy anyway, but Axel has just made my life one hell of a lot easier.

CHAPTER SEVEN

Dash

M Y FAMILY GATHERS around my home, stuck inside because of rainy weather. Which means today isn't as much a barbeque as a get-together, and I've switched the food order accordingly, getting rid of raw meat to barbeque in favor of premade sandwiches. Or rather, Cassidy has.

I've always let my assistant handle the ordering because if I want people to eat and enjoy, I need to let someone else do the choosing. She'd laughed at me since all she had to do was call the store in town that has our standing rain-or-shine order for me or Xander, depending on whose month it was to host.

Everyone is here except Chloe and Beck, who call from the road to say they've hit traffic coming from the city due to an accident.

Prior to today, I have had a solid week in the studio with the band. We've each contributed to the songwriting process, bringing lyrics we've been working on in private, along with melodies and refrains that come to us as we share the words. I love collaborating with my bandmates, and I'm glad Axel contributes to the quality of their music.

We've spent hours jamming, joking, bonding, and yeah, writing solid songs. Although we have a long way to go, I feel good about where we're headed. When a long day of working is over, I usually end up at Cassidy's cozy house and in her bed—and thank God she has a king-size mattress to accommodate my tall frame and lots of amazing sex. But more importantly, we're building a relationship, something I now understand I want for the first time in my life.

During the day, Cassidy acts as the band's assistant, around if I, or any of the guys, need her. She makes sure we have lunch sent in, coffee, sodas, and snacks on hand. In addition, Sasha's production company will be kicking into gear the first of next month. So Cassidy has also begun interviewing people to take her place as the band's personal assistant. Once she narrows down her choices, she'll let the band meet the people she's short-listed and ultimately decide who we want to hire.

I understand Cassidy better now. At night, when I hold her, she talks about her past, and I've had glimpses into her vulnerability due to losing her parents at a young age. I see how me leaving her that morning in the hotel room had dug into an open wound of abandonment. Knowing her issues, I have to figure out a way for her to accept my touring lifestyle without triggering her again.

On a more basic level, I've learned she likes her coffee light with no sugar, a basic healthy turkey on whole wheat with tomato for lunch, and that cooking isn't her thing; it's more mine. She usually orders in and has dinner waiting when I come over between seven and eight p.m. That has become our get-to-know-you time.

The more I learn, the harder I fall. It hasn't taken long and maybe it doesn't need to. Chloe and Beck met the night of her almost-wedding and have been inseparable ever since. The thought brings me back to my first night with Cass at the hotel room all those months ago. Because I'd woken up and my first thought had been about rolling over, holding her, and taking her again, I freaked out.

Which is what sent me running, and though I've learned my lesson, I don't know what will happen when the band begins to travel and Cassidy's job ramps up. But I'm grateful for now. And always aware something could happen to make the new life that I'm trying to build come crashing down. Like telling Cassidy about Billy.

"Hi, honey." My mother walks up to where I stand looking out the window into the rain.

I've been so engrossed in the memories, I've all

but forgotten about my family around the room. "Hi, Mom." I give her a kiss on the cheek.

"What's got you so lost in thought?" she asks.

I shake my head and grin. Leave it to my mom to pick up on the fact that I wasn't watching the rain, that I'd been in deep reflection.

I shove my hands into my pants pockets. "Just thinking about life."

She rolls her eyes. "Maybe you were. Or maybe you're thinking about that beautiful blonde over there holding your niece. Isn't my grandbaby adorable?"

I love how my mother thinks of Aurora's daughter as her grandchild. She's such a warm, giving woman and I know how lucky we all are to have her as our mom.

I turn my gaze in the direction my mother was tipping her head, and my heart catches in my throat. Cassidy sits on the sofa, Aurora's infant, Leah, in her arms. She's talking to my sister, her eyes sparkling with happiness, her face lighting up every time she glances at the baby.

I swallow hard.

"Now, now. Don't pass out on me," Mom says, chuckling.

"No hyperventilating, believe it or not." At one time I would have done just that, and I actually came close when Daisy Masterson accused me of fathering her baby.

The thought of Cassidy and my kid? I'm not ready to be a father yet, not by any stretch of the imagination, but when the time is right? Yeah, I think I want a family someday. With her.

"I never thought I'd see that look on your face for any woman," my mom muses. "It's good, Dash. I'm happy for you."

"Thanks."

She steps closer, her shoulder touching my arm. "So … I know the anniversary of Billy's death is this week, and I wanted to make sure you were okay?"

That's my mother, always supportive. She calls every year at this time or corners me alone to check on my mental state.

"I'm fine. Really. The band is doing a meet and greet at the Hamptons Rehab Center tomorrow. Doing outreach always helps center me."

She nods. "Good. I'm glad I don't have to worry about you."

I shrug. "I can't help but always feel guilty about what Dad did for me… On the other hand, I wouldn't be where I am today if he hadn't." It's ironic, really. My father never approved of his son's dreams of being a rock star, but with his actions, he'd freed me to become the man I am today.

"Honey, listen to me. Just know that what your

father did helped Billy's family as much as it did you. And now you're doing what you can to pay it forward." She squeezes my hand. "Stop torturing yourself over what you can't change."

"Yeah." I clear my throat.

"Does Cassidy know?" she asks.

I shake my head. "Not yet but I plan to fill her in."

"Good. I'm sure opening up to her will help you feel better, too."

I'm not so certain.

Before we can continue our conversation, Chloe and Beck arrive, walking into the family room hand in hand. My sister is beaming. Beck might have started out as Linc's former friend and nemesis, but nobody can deny he's the perfect man for our sister.

"We're here!" Chloe says, waving at everyone.

"Glad you finally showed up," Linc says gruffly.

"Traffic was ridiculous." Beck pulls Chloe farther into the room.

"We have news!" Chloe is practically bouncing up and down in her designer shoes.

Our mother raises her eyebrows and starts toward her daughter, but Linc beats her to it. "What's going on?" he asks.

"We're married!" She holds up her hand, revealing a gleaming diamond wedding band alongside her sparkling princess-cut stone. Because that's what Beck calls my sister. Princess.

"Oh my God. You … I mean I didn't get to see you get married." Mom's voice shakes and I wince.

"I'm sorry, Mom. Beck was in Vegas for business, and I was with him. It was a spur-of-the-moment thing because we just wanted it to be official." Chloe grasps our mother's hand. "But we talked about having a second ceremony for family and friends followed by a huge party, if it makes you happy."

Our mother's expression softens. "Honestly, you sort of had a big wedding once, and I don't want to force you into something huge that you don't want."

Chloe hugs her tight before stepping back. "What about a small reception for our families?" she asks.

Mom nods, her eyes brightening. "That sounds wonderful. Do you at least have pictures?"

Chloe smiles, and then she's surrounded by everyone wanting to see the glittering wedding band on her finger and the photos.

I figure I'll talk to my sister and her new husband later. I make my way over to Cassidy, who is still sitting with Aurora, but Cassidy has made the handoff to my sister so she can give the baby her bottle.

"Hi," I say, sitting on the stone coffee table in front of them.

"Hi, yourself." Aurora smiles. "So that was good news, yes?" She tilts her head toward the entry, where

Chloe is surrounded by family.

"I'm glad Mom isn't worked up that her baby girl got married without her there. I feel like we dodged a bullet when Chloe offered a redo."

Cassidy winces. "I can understand where they're each coming from though. After being left at the altar once, I can see why a Vegas elopement was appealing to Chloe."

"True," Aurora murmurs. "But it looks like all's well that ends well, right?"

"Yes," I say, relieved.

"So how is the creative process on the album going?" Aurora asks.

I'm always happy to talk about music. "We were well into our next album when Dominic left. Axel's done his own writing and we're working it in. Another couple of weeks and we could be into the recording stage, as long as our engineer and producer can come out here to work." I prefer to record in my own studio, and I've reached the status where nobody argues with my artistic needs.

"That's amazing! And when you go on tour, will there be another incident like the one where you guys returned to the dressing room to find naked groupies?" Aurora wiggles her eyebrows and I groan.

My face burns with embarrassment that my twenty-year-old sister knows that story and the fact that she's repeated it to Cassidy. "That was Dom's doing, and no, that won't ever happen again." I can't bring myself to face Cassidy after that revelation. "Enough about me. What were you ladies discussing before I walked over?" I ask.

"Girl talk," my sister says, wrinkling her nose.

"As in none of your business," Cassidy says, her tone sounding … off.

Not a surprise given Aurora's topic of conversation about the band. She was joking, not considering how Cassidy might take her words, because she's young and inexperienced.

I hold back a groan, glancing at my sister.

She pulls the empty bottle out of Leah's mouth, sits her up on her knee, and begins to pat her back. My niece lets out a burp any self-respecting teenage boy would be proud of, and I burst out laughing. Both women join in.

"Give her to me," I say, holding out my arms.

Aurora passes her daughter to me, and I cuddle her close to my chest. "Gotta say, you made one pretty girl," I tell my sister.

Nobody knows anything about the baby's father. All Aurora has ever told us was they'd met and shared one night, no last names exchanged. She has no way of finding him and she's accepted that fact.

"I never thought this could be my life." Aurora

gestures around the room. "Family, friends, a roof over my head, and not having to worry every day about food and shelter. I'm so grateful that Linc decided to come find me."

"I'm glad you don't have to worry anymore, too." Cassidy reaches out and squeezes Aurora's hand. "And remember, you're lucky, yes, but you're also deserving. Don't ever doubt it."

I brush a hand over my niece's back, agreeing with all the sentiments exchanged. Whatever problems we have, the Kingstons are a tight unit, and for that, we are all fortunate.

My cell buzzes in my pocket and I hand the baby to Aurora. "Gotta check and see who's calling." I pull out my phone and look at the screen.

Scowling, I accept the call and place the cell to my ear. "What do you want, Dean?" I have put the man out of my mind, and haven't talked to the band about possible changes to management. But I still haven't gotten over how the bastard treated Cassidy, who hears the man's name and frowns.

But she turns away, engaging Aurora in conversation, obviously wanting nothing to do with my asshole manager.

"I've had my assistant tracking the band's social media accounts as well as your personal ones, and you know what she reported back? It's fucking quiet,"

Dean says before I can answer.

I grip the phone harder. "We're in the studio making music. Isn't that what we're supposed to be doing?" I ask, annoyed by the interruption.

"You're also supposed to be keeping the fans interested by posting. Told you to hire a social media consultant and let them run your pages," Dean says.

I glance heavenward. I've already had enough of the man. "And I told you I decide what gets out to the public and what doesn't. Last I heard, the guys said the same thing."

"Well, if you're not in people's minds, they're going to forget about you," Dean says.

I shake my head. "Not fucking likely." Dean is more concerned about his own relevance, and is pushing the band harder because of it.

I'm not worried about our fan base. And since I've stopped posting stupid crap, I've been more relaxed. The last photograph is one of me and Cassidy at the VMAs. I'm not ready to add another.

"I'm going to set up a meet with Misha Raye. She handles the top music accounts," Dean says.

"Don't bother, because we won't be taking the meeting. Now, it's a fucking Sunday, and I have better things to do than waste time with this shit," I say, and disconnect the call.

I wonder if Dean is also bothering Jagger and Mac,

who've gone to visit their own families. Only Axel has stayed, because his sister is here.

I look over to where the man sits with Xander's dog, Bella, petting her head and talking to her as if she were human. Axel seems to have bonded with the golden retriever. He's even gotten into my habit of hanging out at Xander's place during our downtime just to play catch with the dog.

"Problem?" Cassidy asks, telling me she's been paying attention, even as she talked with Aurora.

"Nothing I can't handle. Do me a favor? Don't send Dean the information about the time and place of the meet and greet. I don't need him up my ass there."

"Okay, I won't," she assures me.

No doubt Dean already knows the time is coming since the band does one of these events every fall, and I've occasionally had our assistant set up visits in a couple of states if we're on tour. Dean pushes for publicity; I refuse. And I've never told our manager why this is something I need to do in private. If Dean digs deep enough, he'll figure it out, but so far he hasn't disrespected the boundary I've set. And by the grace of everything in the universe, nobody else has dug up the dirt on my past. No doubt due to my father's money and influence at the time.

"Eew." Aurora's voice interrupts my thoughts. A

glance at my sister shows she's wrinkled her nose in disgust.

No sooner has she spoken than both Cassidy and I do the same as we become aware of the vile smell emanating from such a small baby.

"Jesus," I mutter.

"Comes with the territory," my sister says, laughing.

Not any time soon, I think, but keep that feeling to myself.

Aurora rises to her feet, infant in her arms. "I left my baby bag in one of the guest rooms. I'm going to go change her."

"Put a towel down on the bed in addition to that narrow plastic thing," I tell her.

Aurora laughs. "Yeah, yeah. Don't worry. I know what I'm doing." She walks away, leaving Cassidy grinning at me.

"What?" I ask.

She shakes her head. "Your reaction to a dirty diaper is priceless."

"That shit scares me," I mutter.

"Pun intended?" she asks.

I laugh. Making a quick switch, moving from the table to the space beside Cassidy, I hook an arm around her and pull her in for a brief kiss. One I hope will reassure her as best I can, at least for now.

★ ★ ★

Cassidy

THE KINGSTONS ARE … a lot, I think. Although I love them and appreciate how they treat me like I belong, the loud din of so many voices over too many hours has gotten to me. As I told Dash, I'm not used to a large family.

I need some time alone to destress and unwind. Aurora has mentioned Dash touring at some point in the near future, and the thought has set off all my internal alarms about men and being left behind. Out of sight, out of mind had certainly been Adam's MO, and he hadn't even been a rock star with women at his beck and call on the road.

Speaking of groupies, that story about naked women in the dressing room has also shaken me. The guys are close. I have a feeling what happens on the road stays on the road. My only saving grace will be that her brother is there and won't protect Dash at my expense. But I don't want Dash behaving just because he doesn't want to get caught. I want him to want me and only me.

To be fair, we haven't had a conversation about the future, and even I know it's too soon. But the thought has settled in the back of my brain, and I fear it will stay there. As if he senses my distress, he kisses me, and when I lift my head, I see my brother watching us, concern on his face.

And if those incidents aren't enough, Dash has to go and hold Aurora's baby. The infant's pale skin cradled in his tanned, tattooed arms also shakes me. My God, I'm not ready for a family, yet my ovaries nearly explode at the sight. It's something I'd love to have someday with Dash. But I just freaked out about the temptations on tour. It's all overwhelming.

Using the excuse that I have a headache, which isn't totally a lie, I tell Dash I'm going home for the night, and leave before the last of his family disperses. He's surprised when I say goodbye, but I need space.

Once home and soaking in the claw-foot tub that was a draw when I decided to rent this house, I lean back and close my eyes, trying to push aside all the questions about Dash—his intentions and, more importantly, his ability to remain committed to one woman for the long haul—that run through my mind in a never-ending loop.

That fails miserably, so I let my thoughts wander. Yes, the parties in his house stopped the day he found out he wasn't going to become a father, and if Jagger and Mac want action, they go into town at night. With Labor Day over, the Hamptons have emptied out, and as winter comes closer, I don't know how happy the guys will be here and not in the city. My brother hasn't said a word about remaining in the beach town and whether or not he'll feel isolated after his time in LA.

But after they finish the album, they'll go on tour. That's what bands do. They write, they put out their music, they tour. And enjoy everything that goes along with the lifestyle of a rich and famous playboy rock-and-roll star. I've seen it with my brother and his old band, and I've heard the Kingstons talking about Dash's behavior before the paternity test came back.

I'm not insecure nor do I have low self-esteem. I am, however, a realist. And two weeks of playing boyfriend and girlfriend doesn't make for a relationship that will last. Even if we continue getting to know each other, me falling harder for him every day, how can I know he's a man I can put my trust and faith in?

I sigh. Worrying won't change anything, and the band going on tour is a long way off. Right now, I just need to focus on my own life, which includes hiring a new assistant for the band and getting up to speed with Sasha on my new job.

I finally notice the water has cooled. I unplug the drain and climb out, wrapping myself in a fluffy towel. After drying off, I dress in a pair of soft shorts and a loose cropped top.

I'm about to heat up some leftovers when my doorbell rings. Expecting it to be Dash, I draw a deep breath and stride to the door, surprised when I see my brother waiting outside.

I open the door and meet his gaze. "Hi!"

"Hi, yourself. Got a few minutes?" He folds his arms across his chest and waits.

"For you? Always. Come on in." I wave him over the threshold, and he walks in, heading straight for the kitchen, the place we usually gravitate to when he comes over.

My brother is handsome. With dark blond, nearly brown hair that brushes his shoulders, he possesses a surfer-boy look that women love. If I didn't objectively know that, the girls who have always flocked to him, both in high school and now as a famous rock star, make it clear.

"I was just going to microwave leftover meatloaf. Can I interest you in some?" I ask.

He shakes his head. "I ate plenty of food at Dash's house. You didn't?"

"No. I had a headache and wasn't hungry."

He pulls out a stool at the counter and sits down. "Feel better?"

I nod. "I took a relaxing bath."

He drums his fingers on the counter. "Was it the number of people around or the family vibe that got to you?"

I love my brother because I don't have to dig deep

and reveal my pain. He just gets me, as I do him. "It takes getting used to," I admit.

"And do you need to? Get used to it, I mean. Are you actually trying for a real relationship with Dash?"

I manage a shrug, given how I've just gone over how confused I am myself.

He leans forward on his elbows. "Cass, are you sure you know what you're doing with him?"

"No, I don't." I stand across from him and lean on my elbows, too.

"I warned him not to hurt you or he'd have to answer to me."

I groan. "You don't need to get involved in my love life." Especially because my choices with Dash impact my brother's future with the Original Kings.

"Too late. I knew something real was going on the night you two didn't come home after the awards, and I confronted him when he got home."

I glance up at the ceiling. "You're not my father!"

"I'm all you've got," he oh-so-helpfully reminds me. "You said you're not sure of what you're doing. I get that. You're scared and confused. So back it up. Do you trust him?"

I meet my brother's worried eyes. "I want to. And I know you guys are nowhere near a tour, but Dash has never been on the road with a girlfriend at home before." I bite down on the inside of my cheek before continuing. "I heard stories today about naked women, and I don't want to imagine what else could tempt him." I blow out a long breath. "To be honest, it scares me, the wondering and not knowing. Can he resist temptation? How do I know?" I twist my hands together, and Axel covers them with his own.

"You don't. That's where trust comes in. Look, it's still early days, and like you said, you have more time to learn about the guy. Same for me. I don't know any of 'em well, but I'm working on it."

I nod in understanding.

"And from the way he's looking at you? It doesn't seem like he's anywhere near wanting to end things, which is why I didn't go after him with these." He holds up his fists.

"No, it's because you need your hands to play."

He shrugs. "Whatever. But if I see red flags, you'll be the first to know."

I expel a harsh breath. "Great. My brother is keeping an eye on my…"

"Boyfriend," he says with a grin.

I pull the dishtowel hanging on the dishwasher handle and whip him with the end like we used to do when we were kids. "One thing I promise: I won't let anything that happens between me and Dash affect you and the band. Your future is too important."

"Then I guess we have each other's backs. Like

always," Axel says, his expression soft.

Pushing himself up from his seat, he strides around the counter and pulls me into a hug.

One I need badly.

★ ★ ★

Dash

EVERYONE HAS GONE home, and only Xander and Sasha remain. Axel has left and Sasha is in the kitchen. I hear the water running from the sink. Sasha is probably cleaning up, but it isn't her job. I have a cleaning crew coming in the morning. Xander usually leaves gatherings early because, like Cassidy, large groups of people and crowds get too confining for him, even if they are family. Yet Xander remains seated on my big sofa.

Which means my brother wants to talk.

Resigning myself to … a lecture? A pep talk? I don't know, but I walk over to the taupe couch, plop my ass down, and put my booted feet up on the cocktail table.

Xander raises his eyebrows. "Really?"

I shrug. "My house, my rules." Just like when I sat on it earlier. "So why aren't you home already?"

"Because I wanted to see if you needed anything."

I narrow my gaze.

"Cassidy?" Xander prods. "Sasha and I saw she left early." With a shrug, he also puts his feet on the table.

"She had a headache. I think the whole family in one place, inside with loud noise, is too much for her." I also have a gut feeling Aurora's talk about touring had been the ultimate trigger for her to withdraw.

"Take it from someone who knows. We're a handful." Xander folds his hands across his stomach. "So you two are a real couple?"

I nod. "Trying to be. It started out as a damned good idea, but I knew from the minute Naomi suggested it, Cassidy pretending to be my girlfriend would give me a way back in. One I might not get otherwise. I've been bending over backwards to show her I want to change."

Xander glances at me. "I'm sure it's easy now. We're all living within a mile of each other. It's the travel and issues on the road that you need to consider."

"No shit. Aurora asked about the next tour, and from that moment on, Cassidy was in her own world." I fiddle with a hole in my jeans. "I can change a lot of things. I deleted hookup numbers from my phone and told her, and I can promise not to sign another body part ever again. But I can't change the nomad part of my lifestyle. And that seems to throw her." Which leaves me unsure if I should show up at her place tonight or give her the space she needs.

I'm not concerned about my own behavior. At this point, the thought of hooking up with anyone other than Cassidy turns my stomach. Compared to her, every other chick just seems like a cheap imitation of what a woman should be. I shudder at the thought of the typical groupie who follows the band. But Cassidy is probably worried.

I decide to be honest with my brother. "I haven't been with anyone since Cass that first time."

Xander, who's been pinching the bridge of his nose, probably due to a headache, whips his head around to look at me. "No shit?"

I shrug.

A slow smile spreads across Xander's face. "Then you know what you want, just like I did. Now you have to find a way to make it work."

And Xander would know. He and Sasha had to find serious compromises in order to be together. From each living on a separate coast to her travel for work, not to mention a fucked-up past, they've had their challenges.

"First Cassidy needs to know about me." I pause, drawing a breath. "Tomorrow's the meet and greet at the rehab place in town."

"Anniversary of Billy's death," Xander mutters.

I clench my jaw before managing to say, "Cass's parents were killed in a car accident by a guy under the influence of drugs. Something tells me she might not want to cut me any slack."

Xander winces. "I knew they died in an accident, not the details." He rubs his hand along the back of his neck, a signature move when deep in thought.

"She told me when I asked her to set up the event. Nate, the manager, expects the call around this time every year," I say. "He'll gladly work with her."

"Somehow I don't see Cassidy holding anything against you. Most kids do drugs at one time or another. It wasn't your fault you bought bad shit." Xander shrugs, meaning what he says.

I sucked in a breath. "But Dad—"

"Was an asshole most of the time. In this case? I think he did you a favor. Just be honest with her. It's all you can do." Xander slaps his hands on his thighs, drops his feet to the floor, and stands.

I rise, too. "You out of here?"

"I'm tired. My eyes hurt and I want to grab Sasha and go home."

I pull my brother into a one-armed hug. "Thanks, man."

"Always."

I wait until Xander and Sasha have left before pulling out my phone and texting Cass. If she is up for company, I'll spill my guts before tomorrow's event.

How's your head?

I see the dots indicating her typing a reply.

Cass: *A little better. I took some Ibuprofen and I'm already in bed.*

Shit. I know she had a full day and tomorrow will be busy as well. I don't want to overload her with emotional crap when she isn't operating on all cylinders. Besides, I can use the time to figure out what the hell I'm going to say.

I'll let you rest. Talk in the morning? I ask. But I hope she'll tell me to come over anyway, even if it's just to hold her.

Those dots show up again, then I see her delete before she starts typing again.

Cass: *Sounds good. I could use a good night's sleep.*

Fuck. "Sweet dreams," I type, feeling every inch the pussy I'm becoming. All for this one woman who doesn't believe in me.

And that's *before* she learns about my past.

CHAPTER EIGHT

Dash

I LEAVE MY Ferrari in the garage, and the guys load Mac's bass, Jagger's guitar, and Axel's Pearl compact drum kit into the back of my Range Rover. Since Axel can't take his full set, he needs at least his snare drum for the sharp rattle and the heavy boom to keep time.

We'll take requests, play a few songs, and talk to the people who are staying at the center. Inpatient consists of people sixteen and older, and it's the younger kids I like to sit with and tell my story to. My drug use had been recreational, but who knows what could have happened if I hadn't been hit with tragedy?

Given the Twelve Step Program of Narcotics Anonymous and the promise of total privacy, my identity is protected, and I've always felt safe at the center. The people I talk to are just happy to hear they aren't alone and that addiction can happen to anyone in any walk of life.

I might not have become an addict, but I have been forever affected by drugs. My past makes an important point and I need to share it. I find it easier to talk in small groups of like-minded people who won't judge.

The guys pile into the back seat, and Cassidy takes the front for the short ride to the center. I wish Cassidy and I had had time to talk before today's event, but she slept in and arrived at my house in just enough time to leave.

She seems brighter this morning than she did when she left my house yesterday, and I don't sense her retreating emotionally. She even caught me alone in the kitchen and greeted me with a long, sweet kiss.

Maybe she'd just needed a night to herself, and doesn't everyone deserve one of those? I know her reasons were because of the conversation about the tour and the groupies, and it's something I can talk to her about later.

We arrive at the center, a beautiful building with well-maintained landscaping. I know from past visits there are gardens in the back with benches to sit on and pathways to walk.

Everyone except Axel has done these with me before, and when I asked the newest member to donate his time, I got no pushback. Axel wants to fit in with the band and so far, so good.

I park close to the building. We all climb out of the Rover, doors slamming as we exit. While the guys collect their instruments, I come around to Cassidy's side, meeting up with her after she steps out. Then I head to the back and grab bags filled with promotional items for signing and giving away.

The weather has cooled, and my blue Henley is comfortable without a jacket. Cassidy has dressed down, wearing jeans like the rest of the band. Regular clothes to meet regular people. It's the way we prefer to look anyway.

Her dark denim hugs her curves, as does the hunter-green silk top that brings out the jade coloring in her eyes. She's tucked the front into her waistband while the back hangs midway down her ass, and a pair of sexy-as-fuck heels completes the outfit.

Realizing I'm ogling her, I turn my head, but not before I see her grin. "See something you like?" she asks.

"Everything," I reply in a husky voice, pulling her against me. "I missed you last night." I've spent so many nights in her bed, I had a hard time sleeping without her wrapped around me.

"I should have asked you to come over," she admits.

"Why didn't you?"

She tips her head back to meet my gaze. "Truth? I wanted to prove to myself I could sleep without you and be fine."

She doesn't say it, but I hear the words *just in case* at the end of that sentence. Just in case I get freaked and end things? In case I hook up with someone else? In case … I could go on and on.

And *ouch*.

That bit of honesty stings. "How'd that work for you?" I ask.

She raises and lowers her shoulders. "Not so well. I missed you."

I release the breath I've been holding. I wind her hair around my hand and tug so her neck bends back and her gaze locks with mine. "Next time, you talk to me instead of trying to prove a goddamned point that tortured us both."

"Hey! Let's go, lovebirds," Jagger yells out. "We've got places to go and people to see."

I glance over to see Axel rolling his eyes and hear Mac laughing out loud.

I tug on Cassidy's hair again. "We're not finished discussing this." I release my grip on the long strands. "Coming!" I call back.

I grab her hand and start toward the guys.

She attempts to tug out of my grasp. "I'm working. It doesn't look professional if we walk in like a couple."

"Us kissing just now wasn't professional and you're my girlfriend." I sulk and she laughs.

Besides, I have a point. "Don't pout. Come on." She pulls me toward the front entrance, dropping my hand at the same time I catch sight of Dean standing by the doors.

Sunglasses on, his shirt unbuttoned on top, sleeves rolled, as he taps something on his phone, he looks like the important man he was. He just isn't needed here.

"Who the fuck told him where we'd be?" I ask.

"Not me," Cassidy says. "You said you didn't want anyone to know."

Jagger and Mac answer at the same time. "Not me."

Axel groans. "Sorry, man. Dean called me and asked when the annual meet and greet was scheduled. Nobody told me not to say anything."

Of course Dean has gone around the original guys who already know the drill and understand this is personal to me, while Dean would try and weasel publicity out of it.

"Not your fault," I say to Axel. I'd forgotten the new band member needed a warning and should have known Dean would be underhanded.

Dean pushes off the wall he's been leaning against and walks over. "Hey, guys. Good to see you," he says, shaking everyone's hand. And ignoring Cassidy.

I grit my teeth as I take my turn, my gaze narrowed

until Dean gets the message and turns to her. "Hello, Ms. Forrester."

"Mr. Jerome." She acknowledges him just as coldly, with a curt nod.

Dean glances at me. "I thought you preferred this to be a private event. No need for a fake girlfriend here." He lifts his eyebrows, his gaze on Cassidy. "It's unnecessary if you ask me."

"I didn't ask your opinion or invite you here. I thought I made myself clear about pushing your own agenda?"

Before Dean can reply, Cassidy clears her throat. "I need to go inside and check in with the supervisor. Nate said he'd send guys out for the equipment once we arrived."

I squeeze her shoulder.

Turning, she walks through the doors into the center.

Axel steps up to Dean. "What the fuck is going on with you and my sister? You have a problem with her?"

I've been waiting for her to disappear inside before I have it out with Dean. Her brother beats me to it.

Dean slips his cell into his pocket. "What makes you say that?"

"Don't treat me like I'm stupid. But assuming *you* are, I'll lay it out for you. The chill in the air, the last names, you asking why she's here, and the disgusted look on your face. Need more?" Axel steps farther into the man's personal space. "She's the band's P.A. She belongs here."

Not wanting a scene at this place in particular, I put a hand on Axel's shoulder, hoping to calm him down.

"As an assistant, I understand. But I saw them making out in the parking lot. And I just happen to think a celebrity girlfriend would do more to push Dash's status as a reformed playboy and keep him in the news. Which means the band is in the news and you boys get more play."

Asshole that he is, Dean clearly hasn't read the room, and Axel looks like he is about to explode.

Having been in the man's position and knowing that ignoring Dean is best, I look to my drummer. "Come on. We have better things to do than listen to his bullshit opinions."

Axel storms away, swinging the door open and walking inside. I follow, catching up to him, Jagger and Mac on my heels.

I pause, turning to the guys. "We need to have a meeting about him. I'm not happy and I need to know if he's who you all want guiding us going forward." I gesture toward the door, where they can see through the glass to the sidewalk where Dean still stands. He's obviously made or taken a phone call. "But not now. I need focus for the people waiting to meet us."

"We'll talk but I'm sure we're on the same page," Jagger says.

"We have your back and know you have ours." Mac's voice is solid.

I nod and turned to our drummer. "Axel. You need to know I have hers," I say, talking about his sister.

The woman I have deep feelings for. Deep enough that I'm about to tell her everything I'm ashamed of doing when I was younger.

But first I have people to meet, talk to, and support.

★　★　★

Cassidy

THE SUNROOM OF the rehab center acts as an auditorium. Dash and the band are in front of windows. I find the view of the lush, green outdoors beautiful. Despite the small area, they're still set up in band formation. Amps are stacked with attention to not covering vents. The guitar speakers are on the opposite side of the drums. Bass traps are set up along with a drum shield to reduce bass frequency and drum reverberation. In a small room, no one wants to cause hearing damage or sacrifice sound quality. All things I've learned from my brother during his musical journey.

The room is filled with people of all ages and genders along with excited whispers and chatter the more crowded it becomes. Nate, the director, is grateful for the band's appearance today and even more appreciative of the one-hundred-thousand-dollar donation Dash has made to each of their five sister centers around New York State.

Five hundred thousand dollars in total. I had no idea he'd done such a thing, and my heart beats harder on hearing it.

I stand in the back of the room beside the director, ignoring Dean, who is chatting up some of the staff nearby. I don't know why the man hates me so much beyond a disagreement or two and the fact that I don't fit the mold of a woman he thinks a man of Dash's status should be with.

Well, he can go fuck himself, I think. I don't appreciate his attitude or how he treats me, and from the way my brother keeps glaring at the man, I'm not alone. I already know Dash has issues with him, too.

I have no say in who the band uses as their manager and understand he'd plucked them from obscurity, helping to get them where they are today. Maybe they feel like they owe him or he's that good at his job, despite his obnoxious personality.

I tell myself that I'll be gone soon, working for Sasha and company, and Dash's need for a fake girlfriend will come to an end. Then it won't matter what Dean thinks about me, so ignoring him is my best option. I rub my chest on the spot above my heart and blow out a long breath in an attempt to calm my racing pulse.

The strum of guitar strings has me glancing toward the stage. Axel cracks his sticks together to count for the band. And then they play. Closing my eyes, I get lost in Dash's baritone, his voice a rich, low texture. He brings an effortless control to his distinctive sound. I tap my foot to the beat as he sings of reaching for the stars and opening up to the universe and its myriad possibilities.

I know the lyrics he's written by heart because I play his music often. Not that I've admitted as much to him. Smiling at the thought, I open my eyes and catch him staring. At me. He snares me in his gaze and a slow smile lifts his sexy lips. One I have no doubt is meant just for me.

Warmth envelopes me and unexpected sexual arousal pulses low in my belly as he continues to sing, that hot stare never leaving my face. Many women think about snagging a rock star, but for now, this man is in *my* bed. I can't help but smile back, at the same moment the band launches into a faster tune. He winks and turns to work the small stage area allotted to them.

After a long set of songs, the entertainment portion of the day comes to an end, and the band is treated to a standing ovation by everyone in the room. The guys put down their instruments and the more informal meet and greet portion of the day begins. People stream up front, creating a line to talk to each of the men who have given their time and energy for a wonderful cause.

Beside me, two women with name tags on their blouses talk in hushed voices, and though I don't mean to eavesdrop, they're too close not to overhear.

"Isn't it amazing that they do this for us every year?" one of the women, who I assume is a nurse or staff member, asks.

"It's bullshit," the other female says, causing me to stiffen in surprise. "They're all using and then they have the nerve to show up here and act like they have something to give back?"

"Heather, come on. Just because they're rock stars doesn't mean that they're using drugs. That's an unfair stereotype."

I agree. I'm aware of Dash's no-drugs-in-his-house rule, one he adamantly enforces, even when the guys throw a party. Axel has never indulged, mostly because he's been too busy trying to make something of himself since we were left alone without life insurance or an inheritance of any kind after our parents, then later our grandmother, died.

I've always admired my brother and feel the same for Dash since I've learned of his similar stance. I also know how hard it must be not to indulge when, as bona fide rock stars, drugs of all kinds are everywhere. Especially when they're on tour.

They are a hazard as much as alcohol. If the man who'd crashed into my parents' car hadn't been high, he wouldn't have been driving the wrong way on a freeway at night, and Axel and I wouldn't have been orphaned. It left me overly aware of how important it was that places like this, where people can get help, exist.

"Well, I happen to know Dash Kingston does use drugs," the woman named Heather says.

Every muscle in my body locks into place. I clench my hands, wondering how the hell she can make such a claim.

"It's so unfair that my brother died and *he* lived. Worse, look at what the universe has given him! Money, fame, and my family was left to grieve." She sniffs and I refuse to turn and look at her, shock holding me in place while they continue their conversation.

I draw short, shallow breaths, telling myself there are two sides to every story and I don't know Dash's.

"I'm sorry, Heather. I know Billy is why you're working here, to compensate for losing your brother," the other woman says. "I wish the band had come on your day off."

"Me too. I usually arrange it that way but we're short-staffed." Heather says something under her breath, then, "This just proves the rich get away with everything."

I don't know what the actual story is with Heather's brother and her link to Dash, but I assume Billy is the friend Dash mentioned the other day. The reason why he performs this meet and greet and gives so much money to the cause. Whatever happened, it probably also explains why he doesn't touch drugs or allow them in his house.

I bite down on the inside of my cheek, wondering if I should warn Dash about Heather's presence and her anger, but even if I wanted to, there's no way to get near him. Not with all the people surrounding him. I'll wait until they finish and he starts walking back here.

Then I'll attempt to talk to him.

Dash

I'M FEELING GOOD about the event and the people I've seen and spoken to today. There are a few younger patients, of whom many seem to have dual issues, including depression and anxiety. They'll get the treatment they need here, for which I'm grateful. I sign more posters and other goodies and hours have passed. I am beyond ready to head home. Nate's staff is supposed to have loaded the SUV with the amps and the rest of our shit. Since someone has returned my car keys, I assume the job is done.

The room is finally emptying out, and Cassidy waits by the door. I saw her earlier, watched her while I was singing. Once I found her in the audience, I couldn't look away. With her eyes closed, she looked like an angel absorbed in my words. My voice. My music.

Just like I'm absorbed in her. From the second I laid eyes on her, she drew me in. My fear gone, all I want now is to wrap myself around her and never let her go. Too bad she's completely skittish and distrusting.

"Dash!" She waves, rushing toward me.

"Cass, what's wrong?"

She grasps my arm. "We need to talk. There's a woman who knows you and she's been talking about you. She said—"

"You have some nerve showing up here year after year." A woman I recognize steps in front of me, cutting off what was no doubt Cassidy's attempt to warn me.

I close my eyes and groan. "Heather."

"Wow. You remember my name. I damn sure hope you remember my brother's because it's your fault he's dead!" she says, her voice loud.

Murmurs rise around us and people turn to stare.

I ignore the audience. I understand her anger, and there is nothing I can say to make things better. "I'm here because of Billy."

"Don't say his name," Heather spits.

Cassidy looks back and forth between us, and I hate that she's finding out this way. I wish I'd seen her and been able to explain last night, before … *this*.

"Come on, Dash. Let's just go. Before there's a bigger scene." Cassidy grabs my hand and tugs.

Knowing she has a point, I follow her toward the door and out into the hallway that will take us to the exit. I don't see the rest of the band and assume they're already outside. I need air and can't wait to join them.

But when I step out of the building, instead of space, I'm hit with paparazzi calling my name and taking pictures. "Son of a bitch." This is supposed to be an under-the-radar event but it's fucking obvious who's tipped them off.

I pull Cassidy against me and look around for the guys, catching sight of them surrounded and answering questions, pissed-off looks on their faces.

"Dash, rumor has it you've been doing this for years. Why is this cause so important to you?" a man calls out.

"Dash, does this have anything to do with Dom and his drug issues?" a woman asks.

I grit my teeth. Dom hasn't discussed his issues with me or any of the other guys, and the reporters sure as hell don't know anything for sure. He isn't even taking my calls.

My best bet is to ignore the paps and head to the car. Make no statement. Let them take photos. I don't give a shit.

I wrap an arm tighter around Cassidy.

"Dash, is this relationship serious?" someone asks.

I tip my head close to her ear. "We're going to make a run for the SUV," I tell her.

She nods.

"Oh, this is great. More publicity about the great Dash Kingston."

I wince as Heather's voice rings out.

The press or whatever they call themselves grow quiet, sensing a story, and I brace myself for the worst.

I turn to see Billy's sister, arms folded across her chest, glaring at me from where she leans against the building's façade. "Maybe to the world you're a hot-shit rock star, but to me and my family you're the lowlife who bought the drugs that killed my brother."

Cassidy stiffens and everyone around us takes a moment to process her words.

I don't wait. I use their shock to my advantage. "Let's go." I start to walk away, my strides long and fast, Cassidy right beside me.

My movement breaks the silence, and the paparazzi follow us to the vehicle, yelling questions and no doubt snapping pictures of my escape. Apparently the guys followed my lead because they show up seconds later.

I have the keys and hit the key fob, unlocking the doors and giving them an opportunity to climb in and shut out the commotion.

"Jesus. They're like vultures," Jagger says from behind me.

"Fucking animals," Mac mutters.

I hope all the equipment has been loaded, but if not, I don't care. Someone can return for it later. I start the engine and put the car in drive, slowly easing out of my parking spot.

The paparazzi get the hint and turn back toward the rehab center, and in the rearview mirror, I catch sight of Heather talking to a group of people, no doubt giving them the story of a lifetime.

★   ★   ★

Cassidy

I WALK INTO the room with bottles of beer fresh from the fridge and pass them out to the guys. This is my second trip because I can only hold so many bottles in my hands. Dash paces back and forth, crossing the length of his huge family room, over and over again. Jagger, Mac, and Axel have spread out on the sofa and oversized club chairs.

Since our return from the rehab center, Dash had been quiet. The rest of the band takes their cue from him and waits, either for Dash to explode or to chill out. Even I don't know which one to expect.

I have questions. So many questions, as Heather's words ring in my ears. But until Dash and I are alone, I won't press him for an explanation, though I do wonder if the rest of the band already knows the story. Not Axel, since he is as new as I am, and whatever is in Dash's past, that's personal and private.

At least it had been. Until now.

"Who wants to guess who the fuck alerted the press? Because I sure as hell know." Dash finally asks as he picks up a vase and throws it against the wall.

In shock, I watch it shatter.

"Dude, chill. I've left a message for Naomi," Jagger says.

Ignoring him, Dash says, "I want Dean held responsible."

Jagger blows out a breath. "I wouldn't put it past that slimy bastard to out you but maybe we need to consider all options. Just playing devil's advocate here, but could it have been your friend's sister?"

"I doubt it," I murmur. "She's a nurse and respects the Twelve Steps."

"But she could be pissed enough to let her emotions override rational thought?" Jagger raises an eyebrow.

Dash spins to face me. "Who do *you* think it was?"

He obviously trusts her judgment and I appreciate that fact. I also agree with him. "I think it was Dean."

"No wonder the prick disappeared." Mac's disgust with the manager is evident in his frown, before he takes a long sip of his beer.

"That motherfucker is gone," Dash says. He glances at his bandmates, one by one. "Jagger, do you have an issue with it?"

The bassist shakes his head. "No. I just wanted to lay out another option. Dean's been a pushy pain in the ass lately. I'm ready to part ways."

"Same." Mac puts his empty bottle on the table.

Dash's gaze lands on Axel.

My brother nods. "He's never been my guy."

Dash leads the band, but even in the midst of his anger, he turns to the others for a fair decision. His actions show the kind of man he is inside and I admire that.

"I'm firing him in person," he says. "I want to see his expression when he loses the Original Kings." He picks up the beer he'd put on a shelf earlier and takes a long swig, swallowing and drinking some more.

I hate that I have to speak up again, but I can't help it. Someone needs to look out for him. "I don't know the full story, but it sounds like something you're going to want to get in front of," I say to Dash. "I know Jagger said he left your publicist a message, but I'm also pretty certain Heather has already given her version to the press and …"

Dash meets my gaze, and my voice trails off, disturbed by his taut expression and the cloudiness in his eyes that can only be caused by sadness. "Everyone out."

"What?" I ask.

"Not you." He turns to the guys. "I love you like brothers but I need space. I need to breathe. I need…" He glances at me. "I need you guys to find your own places to live."

Their mouths hang open wide. Not Axel's. I already know he hates living in what he calls a frat house and had been talking to a realtor. But the original guys in the band look stunned. To say Dash has shocked them is an understatement.

"What the fuck?" Jagger asks.

Dash dips his head. "I don't mean you have to go immediately. Except to your rooms. I want to talk to Cassidy. But start looking around. Yeah?" he asks.

Jagger frowns. He hesitates, then shrugs. "Yeah. I get it."

Mac leans back in his seat and nods. "It actually works for me. I can't bring chicks home or bang them in the kitchen here."

I blink. "Really?" *Did he just say that?*

Dash glares at him.

"Read the room," Axel mutters to the bassist.

Jagger merely laughs.

But they all push up from their seats and head out, Axel pausing to raise his eyebrows at me, concern etched on his face.

I meet his gaze and shrug, because I don't know what my talk with Dash will reveal.

CHAPTER NINE

Dash

I ONLY PLANNED to kick everyone out of the family room, not my house, but I've been building to this moment for a while. And though I would have preferred to have done it in a nicer way, after today, I feel like the walls are closing in on me, and I exploded, everything that's been weighing on my chest coming out.

I blow out a sharp breath and turn to Cassidy, who stands silently waiting for whatever I'll do or say next. Although I've made sure we have privacy, being in the center of the house, where anyone can come back out at any time, isn't enough. I'm not sure how she'll take the story, and worse, I don't know how emotional I'll become during the reveal.

Throughout the encounter with Heather and the horrible things she yelled at me, Cassidy never lost her composure. She didn't turn to me with accusations in her gaze. I don't know if her stoicism bodes well for what I have to do.

"Let's go to the bedroom," I say.

Arms folded across her chest, her expression wary, she nods. I place a hand on her back, and we walk across the hardwood floors and turn down the hall to the master. The guest rooms are on the other side of the house, where the guys each have their own room.

We step into my haven. A place where I escape from everyone else in the house when the noise or company becomes too much. I'm not a loner like Xander. I like being around friends and family, but to be creative, I also need quiet.

Cassidy waits as I shut the door behind us. "I love this room," she murmurs. "So masculine but peaceful."

I nod in agreement. "I let Chloe decorate but insisted she run all her ideas by me before she purchased anything."

The black and gray theme could have been morbid, but my sister has good taste. She'd chosen black floor tiles with heavy white grout lines framing them in place. Though dark, she insisted they'd reflect natural light back into the room from the windows, and it helps that the wall behind the bed has a light gray concrete stain to brighten it up, too. Or so my sister explained.

"I'll tell her you approve," I say.

"Please do. Maybe one day I'll buy my own place and use her to decorate."

I freeze at her comment and don't like the emptiness that fills me at the thought of her buying a house of her own.

"Dash?"

At the sound of my name on her lips, I refocus. "Yeah. I'm just getting my thoughts together." I gesture for her to take a seat on my platform bed.

She kicks off her heels and settles cross-legged on the gray comforter, then pats the mattress for me to join her. I figure this will be easier if I'm sitting, too. I remove my shoes and sit, turning so we're face-to-face.

Her silence unnerves me, but I know she's waiting until I'm ready. "I don't know where to start."

"How about the beginning," she suggests in a non-judgmental tone.

I nod. "Right. The beginning." I close my eyes and mentally travel back to my late teenage years. "I was seventeen and we'd already put together the beginnings of a band. I went to school with Jagger and Heather's brother, Billy Cooper. We'd hang out in one of our houses and play cover songs. My house was the biggest, so we had the most room to practice." I snort at that. "But I told you when Dad was home, he was an asshole. He didn't want to be bothered by the *noise* we made."

It was her turn to snort. "You mean the music you made."

I can't help but grin. "I wish I'd had you as my defender back then."

She smiles. "What about your siblings? Were you all as close back then as you are now?"

I pause in thought. "We were growing up, dealing with our own shit. Linc was already finishing his MBA and getting ready to follow in Dad's footsteps, joining the family business. Xander had joined the Marines, and Chloe was navigating her early teens. Close came later. Though before Xander took off, I used to be up his ass. I'd sleep on his bedroom floor and drive him crazy."

She laughs, leaning forward and placing a hand over mine. "I see how you land at Xander's house more than your own. He's all bark, no bite and loves having you there. Axel's followed in your footsteps. He's bonded with Bella."

"He loves that dog. Did you have one growing up?"

She shakes her head. "Gran was allergic."

"Maybe one day you will."

She shrugs. "It's Axel who's the dog person and you're changing the subject." She wags her finger at me and I grab it in one hand. Bringing it to my lips, I nip the tip, and her gaze jerks to mine, eyes dilated. "Now you're trying to distract me."

Her perky nipples tell me I've done a good job, but

she's right. I need to face this.

I release my hold. If she still wants to be with me after she learns about that night, I'll be damned lucky. "We usually ended up hanging out at Billy's instead. Billy's dad was the janitor at school, and his job enabled him to put his son in a better school district. The point is, they didn't have much and their house was in a lower-income area."

She purses her lips. "Easier access to drugs," she finally says.

I shrug. "With money, I could have gotten anything I wanted, but yeah, the guys who hung out in the town where Billy lived made it easier."

"Why? You had wealth, friends, a band, talent…"

"A father I hated, the brother I was closest to was in the Marines. I was young, stupid. I thought smoking and drugs made my voice sound better, cooler. Mom didn't realize what I was doing, and I made sure I came home and went straight to my room. No interacting with either her or Dad if he happened to be home."

Cassidy listens intently, her warm gaze on mine. "What happened?"

I press my palms against my burning eyes. "The night Billy … died, I bought coke for the first time and brought it over. His parents weren't home and we were in the garage, where we practiced. He used it immediately. No idea why I didn't. When he passed out, he started seizing and frothing at the mouth."

I shudder at the reminder of my friend, face white, lying on the floor, foam dripping from his mouth, and me, alone because Jagger hadn't been able to come over, frozen in fright.

Cassidy edges closer on her knees, wrapping her arms around me tight.

Shit, I didn't expect that. I've only been holding it together because she's been across from me, at a distance. But enveloped in her warmth, I let go and began to shake as the memory of my friend dying slams into me.

I force myself to go on. "I dialed 911 and did everything they told me to while I waited for them to show up. They tried Narcan and rushed him to the ER." My voice catches in my throat. "I barely remember calling home. Mom answered but my father showed up instead."

Cassidy stiffens but she never releases her hold, as if she knows she is all that is keeping me upright. "What happened?"

"Turns out the coke was laced with fentanyl, something we found out later. My father ... at the time I thought, man, he stepped up, but as I got older…"

She slowly releases her hold and grasps my hand instead. "Go back and explain, okay?"

I nod. "My father took me home. I guess the cops went to the hospital, and by then Billy's parents were there. He was gone." My eyes burn like hell. "They didn't know we were together for sure, but it wasn't hard to figure out. Billy and I were always hanging out. The cops came by my house to talk. My father told them I was sleeping and he'd bring me to the station tomorrow."

"With a lawyer," she murmurs.

Smart girl. "I didn't know it until later, but my father went to talk to the Coopers. He knew that Billy was the only person who knew I bought the coke and Billy was gone. So Dad told his parents that Billy purchased the drugs." Something else I have to live with. "And when Dad came home, before I gave my statement, he instructed me to tell the exact same story."

"So the police wouldn't hold you responsible in any way."

I nod and clench my jaw so hard I'm surprised I don't crack a tooth. "This way he protected the family name."

"And you," she reminds me.

"Maybe that was his reasoning, maybe not." But I have always had my doubts about my father's motives and what was important to him. "He gave Billy's parents money in exchange for them promising they'd never give an interview or discuss me in any way. They agreed. In writing."

Cassidy's eyes are open wide and I can't blame her. I'm still horrified by the fact that my father buried my massive error in judgment with cold hard cash.

"I wonder if Heather knows about the money or the agreement," Cassidy says.

I shrug. "Either way, my father's dead and I'm sure as hell not going to force her into silence. But she is a nurse at the rehab. Somehow she paid for her schooling." I shake my head. "It doesn't matter. Billy died, my father covered up my role in it, and I went on to become a world famous rock star. How is that fair?"

She scrambles to her knees, facing me. "Listen to me. Kids make mistakes and that's what you were. Not an adult, but a child … still learning. It's not your fault that Billy died. It's whoever tampered with the drugs. You can't blame yourself."

"But I can blame my father."

"For what? Protecting his son?" she asks.

"Protecting himself and the family name. I was a secondary thought." And I've always resented my father for that.

Cassidy places her hands on my shoulders. "Maybe, maybe not. But his actions allowed you to live your life. And in doing so, you didn't forget your friend. You fund rehab centers, you do meet and greets to help addicts gain strength and not feel so alone. *You give back.*"

Listening to her defend me feels good. "You sound like my mother," I say.

Cassidy treats me to a warm smile. "Well, she's a wise lady."

I believe the words more coming from Cassidy than I ever have from my own mother, yet I can't help but ask, "Even with how your parents died? You don't think I share the blame for Billy's death?"

She meets my gaze, her expression honest. "No, I don't. You didn't force him to do anything. And if you've been torturing yourself with this for years, you need to stop."

I run a hand over my hair. "Mom calls what my father did my second chance."

Cassidy nods in agreement. "And it's one you've used to do good. I'm sure it's what Billy would have wanted."

"Tell that to Heather," I mutter.

Cassidy shakes her head. "I'm telling it to you because it's true and you need to believe it.

And then she straddles me and seals her lips over mine.

Cassidy

MY HEART BREAKS for the boy who hadn't yet been a man when his best friend died. And his father's actions, well-meaning or not, have left Dash feeling responsible for Billy's death. I hate seeing Dash broken and hurting and want nothing more than to take his pain away.

The moment our mouths connect, he thrusts his hand into my hair and kisses me back like he needs me to breathe. I'll do anything I can to make this moment easier, even allowing him to lose himself in my body.

After watching him perform, I'm on edge, my pulse pounding to the beat of the music, my blood hot from his voice flowing through me. If not for Heather's interruption, I would have jumped him the moment we got home and I'd gotten him alone.

But that would have been a hot moment of sex because I've been so turned on. Now it's more, because I'm willingly allowing my emotions to be involved. Refusing to question myself or bring up all the reasons giving in to my feelings is a bad idea, I slide my fingers through his hair and tug, kissing him with everything I possess.

A deep rumble comes from his chest, and he pulls away, only to reach for the neck of his shirt with one hand and yank it over his head.

"I need to feel your skin against mine," he says, going for my buttons next.

His fingers are large and it takes longer than I would like, but I can't deny how sexy it is to watch him undress me. His big, tanned hands fumbling with the tiny buttons, finally making progress.

I shimmy the silk over my shoulders and the blouse falls onto the bed. His gaze drops to the swells of my breasts, and I quickly unhook my bra, letting it join the pile of clothes on the mattress.

His gaze never leaves mine as he rises and undoes his jeans, stripping naked. Maneuvering on the bed, I manage to do the same, desire a living, pulsing thing inside me.

I urge him to stretch out, patting the pillows lined up along the headboard. His abs flex and muscles move until he's propped against them, his thick cock standing at attention, waiting for me to taste.

And I lean down to do just that.

"What are you doing?" he asks in a desire-roughened voice.

I look up at him. "You're stressed and I'm about to give you the release you need so you can relax."

"You being here makes things better."

And I know by the intense look on his face, he means what he's saying.

My gaze never leaving his, I lean over and lick at

the creamy pre-come on the head of his cock, and he lets out a low groan.

"But I'm not coming alone," he says.

I raise my eyebrows, unsure what he intends. I don't have to wait long to find out. He knifes up, showing the utter perfection of his abs, grabs me beneath the arms, and pulls me against him. My breasts press against his chest, and he buries his head in the nook of my shoulder and neck, shuddering as we cling together.

"Skin to skin, remember?" he asks.

His solid body aligns with mine, and that warm contact is everything I hadn't known I needed.

"Better," he murmurs.

"Much," I agree, savoring the long hug.

He eases back, his hands on my forearms. "Now, stretch out, put your sexy pussy by my face, and you can do what you want to me ... *there*." He gestures to his thick erection, his husky tone all but daring me to do as he asks.

Knowing what's in store for me if I listen, I shift and slide down so I'm looking at his erection and he has access to my needy sex. Before I can grasp his cock in my hand, he slaps one side of my ass, the sting a shock to my system. One that soon turns to a warm burn of need when he smacks the other cheek, then presses his cooler hand to my sensitive flesh.

"Are you good?" he asks, kissing first one cheek, then the other, soothing the sting.

Am I? He's taken me off guard, but a simmering heat dances between my thighs and moisture pools there. "Yes. I'm good."

With a little maneuvering, I get into a comfortable position and take him into my mouth at the same time his tongue licks over my sex. *Oh, God.* I arch toward him, shamelessly asking for more, and he willingly complies.

How am I going to focus on him when he's started sucking and licking everywhere and the warm, wet slide of his lips feels so good? But I'm nothing if not determined, and I grasp his length and suck him in deep.

He stiffens and his hips jerk forward, the head of his cock nudging the back of my throat. I do my best not to gag and manage to swallow around him, causing the hottest sound to reverberate through him.

Before I can lick and entice him with my tongue, he slips two fingers inside me and begins to suck and nibble on my clit. He pumps those long digits, pausing for effect until I writhe in empty agony, only to lick all around my sex, teasing me before filling me again with those fingers and tugging my clit with his teeth.

May climax takes me by surprise, and I forget everything but the waves of pleasure taking over and consuming me as I grind myself against his mouth, looking to eke out every last second of gratification.

I let my body relax long enough to come back to myself before retaking his cock in my hand to return the favor. One I instigated and he's somehow taken over.

I want this to be about Dash and what he needs. So I lean in and suck him back into my mouth. I wrap my hand around the thick base of his erection and slide my tongue along his length.

"Fu-u-uck," he says, pushing deeper.

I pump my hand and swirl my tongue, over and over, repeating the dual motions until he's pumping in and out while I slide my grip up and down. His cock is hard, his entire body rigid, the sounds coming from him utterly arousing.

Suddenly he yanks himself out of my mouth. "Not coming this way when I could come in your pussy. Now get up here so I can fuck you properly."

I shake my head and grin, getting used to his dirty talk during sex. I push myself up, and no sooner have I settled against the pillows than he comes over me, bracing his hands on either side of my head.

His gaze rests on mine, warm and full of an emotion that frightens me, because it's everything I've wanted.

"I appreciate my mother and siblings, and I know

the guys have my back. But nobody outside of family, real or the band, has ever been there for me the way you have," he says.

I touch my forehead to his. He deserves it but I don't know how to express myself without revealing too much.

"I'm falling for you, Cassidy Forrester."

I blink in surprise, my entire body softening at words I never thought I'd hear from my *fake rock star boyfriend*. But then from the beginning, he's been trying to get me to see that we could be *more*.

"Don't freak out on me, babe."

I manage a smile. "I thought I was supposed to be the one reassuring you."

"You have been." He runs a hand over my hair, running his fingers through the strands. "You listened to me, you *heard* me, and you didn't judge. Then you put your hot mouth over my—"

Laughing, I cover his lips with my hand. "Don't ruin the sweet moment."

He licks my palm and my laughter turns to a giggle.

"Grab a condom from the drawer."

I've been feeling his hard length pressing insistently against my stomach, and now that he's all but drawn my attention to it, desire and need return.

I edge closer to his side of the bed, pull out the drawer, and come back with a foil packet in my hand. I rip it open. Taking the condom in one hand, I raise his erection in the other and slide the protection over his rigid length.

"Now move to the middle of the bed and lie down."

★ ★ ★

Dash

I'M MORE THAN ready to fill her and feel her, warm and wet, pulsing around me. To show her with my body what I'm feeling with my heart, even if she isn't ready to hear or believe the words.

She lies back against the pillows, her gaze watchful but her body more than ready. I climb between her legs and lower my head, my lips capturing hers in a brief kiss, my cock at her entrance. Holding myself in one hand, I slide my erection back and forth through her slick folds, working her up and arousing her with pressure that has her arching up for deeper contact.

She bends her knees, and I thrust inside with one long stroke. "Perfect," I say on a groan.

"Oh, God, I agree."

I meet her gaze. "I could make it even better." That's what I want. To make everything better for her the same way she does for me.

She raises her eyebrows, a sensual lift to her lips. "I doubt you could feel any better."

"I always did like a good dare." I pull out, amused at her outraged expression. "Flip onto your stomach." It isn't a request.

Wary but obviously willing, she turns over, coming onto her hands and knees, but that isn't what I meant.

Grabbing a pillow, I place it beneath her stomach. "Now drop down and relax."

She rests her belly against the pillow, which has the effect of raising her hips. I come over her from behind, lining myself up and gliding into her slowly. From this angle, it's a tight fit, her snug inner walls gripping me in heat.

"Oh, God, you're right. I feel you so much more this way."

My entire body shudders at her words, and I lower myself on top of her. Keeping my weight off her back, I brush her hair away from her face and kiss her shoulder.

Every inch of her is silky smooth and I can't get enough. I slide my lips up her neck and graze my favorite spot beneath her jaw.

"Dash, I need you." Her raspy voice does nothing but encourage me, and my cock thickens inside her.

"I've got you," I promise, meaning it in more ways than one.

I brace my hands on either side of her and begin a slow thrusting, in and out, that has my eyes rolling back in my head. She's so tight but aroused and takes me easily, and my need ramps up fast. I won't last long, and I want her to come first.

I slide my hand between her and the pillow, finding her clit and pressing down hard. That touch is all it takes for her to roll her hips as she clamps down on my cock, her orgasm washing over her and triggering my own. We come at the same time, my entire being lost inside her.

I'm not sure how many seconds pass as I lay, sweaty and satisfied, on top of her, but when I return to reality, I slide off her with a groan.

She turns on her side to face me. "Wow."

I grin. "Never doubt me again."

She shakes her head and laughs. "Anyone ever tell you that you're cocky?"

"Yeah." I pull her against me. "But you're the only one I ever wanted to impress."

We lay for a long while, silence surrounding us, and I soak in the peace she's helped me find. Because I know, come tomorrow, the media train will be in full force and I'll have to face my past.

And come to terms with my future.

I WAKE UP with Cassidy in my arms, her presence the only thing keeping me sane when I know my phone has to be buzzing off the hook with social media alerts and calls. I turned it off late last night when I'd gone out to retrieve our cells. Yesterday's fiasco has to have been picked up by major news outlets. *Dash Kingston responsible for a man's death, news at noon.*

"Someone's thinking too hard." Cassidy slides out of my embrace and faces me, propping herself up on one elbow. "What's wrong?"

"I was just realizing everything I'm going to have to deal with outside of this room."

Her understanding gaze meets mine. "You can handle it. It's a storm that will blow over. The sooner we get out of bed and face it, the faster that will happen."

"Yeah, but there's no reason we can't delay a little while longer, for this." I pull her on top of me and press my lips to hers, my cock growing immediately hard.

She moans and kisses me back, threading her fingers through my hair, and keeping me in place until a knock sounds on the bedroom door.

"Go away!" I lift my head and yell.

"Come out here. You have company!" I recognize Xander's voice and wonder if my brother is alone or if he's brought the cavalry with him.

"We'd better get dressed," Cassidy murmurs, doing her best to slide out from beneath me.

"Fine." I let out a groan and slip off her, coming to a standing position beside the bed. "We'll be right out," I call to my brother. "Sorry," I say to Cassidy. "But time to face the day."

She stands and pulls my t-shirt over her head. "I'm going to jump in the shower. I'll meet you out there?"

I nod. "Let me take a quick one first." My gaze scans over her, my need as strong as before the interruption. "Wish I could invite you in with me, but we'd never get out there. This way you don't have to rush."

She waves toward the master bath. "Go." She plops back down on the bed, picks up her phone, and begins to scroll through.

I don't ask what she sees. I don't want to know.

After I've showered and kissed my girl, I leave her to clean up. Walking into the kitchen, I find Xander and Sasha and Linc and Jordan, who've obviously come from the city, sitting around the large table. I was right. Part of the cavalry has ridden to my rescue.

"Are things that bad that you thought you needed to be here bright and early?" I immediately walk over to the coffeemaker, pop in a K-cup, and brew myself the dose of caffeine I know I'll be needing.

Linc clears his throat. "We thought you could use

the support."

I carry my mug in one hand, phone in the other, to the table and join them. "Yeah, and despite how I sound, I appreciate it."

"Are you aware of the fallout from yesterday's run-in with Billy's sister?" Xander asks.

I shake my head. "I've been avoiding social media, email, television, you name it."

Xander glances at Linc. "It's bad. Have you looked outside? The paparazzi are lining the street. They're staying off private property for now, but I wouldn't count on that continuing."

I groan. The entire reason I like the Hamptons is the privacy the people here give me.

"Have your manager get security out here, yesterday," Xander says.

I stiffen. "I'm planning on firing my manager the first chance I get. He's the one who notified the paparazzi we were at the rehab center. Until this year, the events have been under the radar, but Dean's been relentless about publicity lately and he showed up." I pause. "And has suspiciously been nowhere to be found since."

"That bastard," Xander mutters. "I'm calling Alpha Security. I'll have someone here soon." He rises and heads to call the firm we both use, me when on tour and Xander when Sasha had a stalker and needed round-the-clock protection.

Xander steps out of the room to make arrangements. I could have easily made the call, but I need my focus on the next steps and appreciate my sibling taking point.

"What's out there?" I ask Linc. "What has Heather revealed?"

Linc leans forward. "She accuses you of dragging her brother into the music scene, into drugs, and told the press that you bought the coke and it's your fault Billy died."

I pinch the bridge of my nose. "So everything I expected."

"Except the payoff," Linc says.

I guzzle my coffee, needing the jolt to function and deal with this. No doubt I have Naomi leaving half a dozen messages on the phone I turned off last night, informing me of everything Linc just has.

"And I'm sure that would go over well. Kenneth Kingston paid off the family of the man who died using drugs purchased by Dash Kingston," I mutter.

"I'm guessing Heather doesn't know about the money or else she'd have informed the media." Linc drums his fingers on the counter. "I can talk to her and facilitate a new deal that ensures she doesn't keep giving interviews and lets this die down."

Jordan puts her hand over Linc's and shoots me a

sympathetic look. I know she means well, but I don't want everyone feeling sorry for me.

"Where's my nephew?" I ask, changing the subject.

"With Mom. She took him overnight," Linc says. "Now focus, Dash. Thoughts on me stepping in?"

"Stepping in about what?" Cassidy asks, joining us in the kitchen.

I rise from my chair, a huge sense of relief filling me now that she's by my side. I hold my seat for her and pull out another for myself. "Linc wants to talk to Heather and basically pay her to stop giving interviews and let things die out."

Cassidy's eyes open wide in surprise. "What do *you* want?" she asks me.

I look at her while I answer. "I don't think any of us should stoop to Dad's level. I should man up and deal with the consequences of both my actions and his."

Approval lights her gaze.

"But I also think I should talk to Heather, face-to-face. Even if she doesn't buy my side of the story, even if she keeps talking to the media, at least I'll have apologized and done what I need to do for myself."

Reaching over, Cassidy grabs my hand and squeezes tight.

Linc rubs the back of his neck. "I can't say I blame you. I wasn't exactly looking forward to cornering the woman and playing bad guy."

"Agreed," Xander says, rejoining us and sitting down by Sasha, who gestures to Cassidy, obviously wanting to talk in private.

"Are you okay?" Cassidy asks me.

I nod. "Go on. I'm fine."

She smiles and rises to her feet. Along with Sasha, she walks out of the room.

"I hope your fiancée isn't planning to tell Cassidy I have too much baggage and she can do better," I mutter.

Xander narrows his gaze. "She can't do better but that's not the point. Whatever Sasha says, she's just looking out for her friend. She wants what's best for her."

"So do I." I slam my hand on the table, knowing full well no sane woman would want to deal with this shit. First the baby mama drama and now this.

Jordan, who's been silent until now, stands and walks over, placing a hand on my back. "Everyone wants what's best for you, too," she says.

I glance up at the woman who's made my brother a more open, warm human being. "I know that."

"Then trust that what's best for Cassidy is you. No matter what anyone else thinks or says." Jordan glances down. "Can I get you another cup of coffee?" she offers.

I blow out a long breath. "Yeah. Thank you." And then I pick up my cell, turn it on, and let the messages and notifications pour through.

CHAPTER TEN

Cassidy

I SIT WITH Sasha on the comfortable sofa in Dash's family room, unnerved by the worried look on my friend's face. Sasha and I have been through so much from when we lived together in a two-bedroom and barely knew each other and later throughout Sasha's rise to stardom. I trust my friend with everything important in my life.

"What's up?" I ask.

Sasha, looking casual in a pair of jeans and a cute red blouse, leans forward. "I know your relationship started out as pretend, but it's so clearly gone beyond. True?"

I have never lied to my friend. "True."

"You two seem close." Sasha fiddles with a bracelet on her hand and I sigh.

"If by close you mean he talks to me about things he might not tell others, then yes. We are." Since I know what this conversation is about, I have no intention of making Sasha work to get information out of me. "Look, I promise you, my eyes are wide open. I realize Dash is going through a period of self-reflection, and I'm not taking anything he says or does to heart."

At least, that's what I want to think, because if he means it that he's falling for me, I'm falling right back.

"Are you sure?"

I manage a smile. "Is anyone sure about anything? All I can tell you is, I'm well aware his intentions are good, but this might be some phase Dash is going through. I mean, first some groupie claims he fathered her child, and now this mess with his past. He's looking to hold on to something."

"And you're worried that something is you?"

I lift my shoulders. "I'd be stupid not to consider it, right?" Before Sasha can reply, I continue. "I just don't want to be hurt if or when he goes on tour and reverts to old behavior."

"I don't want that for you, either. I just wanted to see where your head was at and make sure you're okay."

Not in the least, I think, but there is nothing anyone can do to change the ultimate outcome. Not even my well-meaning best friend.

"Well, I'm here for you. Anything you need, anytime." Sasha leans forward and pulls me into a hug, which I gratefully return.

"Thanks."

The sound of voices has us turning as everyone else walks in from the kitchen. Dash looks tired, and the day has barely started. Sasha and I rise to our feet.

"I've been trying to reach Dean," Dash says. "The bastard's not taking my calls. Where are the guys? I want to know if they've heard from him." He glances toward the hall with the guest bedrooms, where all seems quiet.

"I haven't seen them," I say. "They're probably sleeping in. Do you want me to wake Axel?"

Xander snorts. "No need. He's at my place, hanging with Bella. Do you see what you did?" he asks Dash.

I bite back a grin because Xander always seems put out by the company, but he never asks anyone to leave. Make that rarely. Sometimes I think he enjoys complaining more than he hates the visitors.

Sasha laughs. "I think he took the dog for a walk."

Even Dash manages to laugh. "I'll talk to the band later. Naomi's in LA at the main office, but she wants to talk via Zoom and nail a strategy. I'll find them by the time she's ready." He turns to his brothers, starting with Linc. "You guys staying?"

Linc shakes his head. "We're heading over to Mom's to get the baby before she spoils him."

"Can you really spoil an infant?" Dash asks.

Jordan looks at Linc, the love in her eyes obvious

for all to see. "Ask us that when we can't put him down because she's been holding him all the time," Jordan says, looking back at Dash.

Linc walks over and pats Dash on the back. "I'm proud of how you're handling this."

So am I.

"I'm not sure why," Dash mutters. "I started this mess."

I hate how he's beating himself up for a situation that any teenager could have gotten himself into. "It could have happened to anyone."

"Anyone stupid enough to buy coke from shitty dealers on the street," he says.

Linc shakes his head. "You can't change the past. Just keep moving forward and doing good. It's all any of us can do." He takes Jordan's hand. They say their goodbyes and leave in an obvious hurry to get back to Jasper. I wish them luck getting through the mass of reporters outside.

Dash runs a hand through his hair, messing it more, and glances at Xander. "What about you and Sasha? Are you staying?"

Xander eyes him with concern. "No, but if you need me, just call."

"Or come over to our place," Sasha says, easing the tension.

Xander grabs her hand. "Don't give him any ideas." He turns to Dash. "Remember what I said. If you need me, you call."

"I will."

"Take care, Dash." Sasha kisses his cheek, and I soften toward my friend, who, just minutes before, had been worried about my involvement with him. In her own way, Sasha is looking out for them both.

Sasha waves and walks out with Xander, leaving me alone with the brooding rock star.

"I don't deserve them, you know."

And those words prove me right. He is in self-flagellation mode. Suffering from survivor's guilt. I understand, but he needs to put it behind him, and I'm not sure how to get him to do that.

"Of course you deserve your family. You give as much as they do," I say.

"By doing a couple of meet and greets because I feel guilty that I lived and Billy didn't?" His voice sounds tortured.

I brace my hands on either side of his face. "By being there when they need you. Why do you hang out at Xander's?"

"Because I like bugging my brother."

I shake my head. "Because Xander's a loner, and before Sasha came back, you didn't want him to hole up in his Hamptons retreat by himself. You look out for him. So stop torturing yourself about something you cannot change." I wait for him to nod, and only then do I release my hold.

He begins to pace the floor in front of the door, and I let him do his thing until he spins around. "What did Sasha say to you? Did she tell you I'm a bad bet? To run?"

"What? Of course not." Sasha had told me to be careful, but I'm not about to repeat those words to Dash. Distracting him is in order. Until he truly faces his past and the damage done, and accepts what he can't change, he'll continue to torment himself. "Why don't you try to call Dean again?"

"Good idea." He whips his phone from his pocket and speed-dials the man who is his manager. For now.

★ ★ ★

Dash

AFTER OUR ZOOM call with Naomi, I pace the studio, where the band and I have holed up to talk. During the chat, I had to sit through a reiteration of yesterday's events and suck up Naomi's idea to set things right. I don't want to sit down with an interviewer, friendly or not, but I agree it is the right thing to do. Naomi knows how to juggle the publicity machine for the band, and she's never steered us wrong, so I gave her the go-ahead to set something up. But I still need to know where everyone in the band stands.

I turn to the guys who have always supported me and vice versa, and though new to the group, Axel has been solid since he's joined. Which means I owe them. I need to fix the PR mess I've created along with my own reputation.

I rub my hands on my faded jeans and look at his friends. "Umm … I'm sorry to bring this shit down on the band." I'm not comfortable with serious, emotional conversation with the guys, but this situation is an exception.

"Life happens," Jagger says. "We all know it. None of us are perfect choirboys."

"What he said," Mac mutters.

Axel, who has better reasons than the other men to be wary of me, studies me for a beat. During the video call, Cassidy had sat by my side, and it's obvious she's here as more than the band's assistant.

Though she's doing her job, as evidenced by the sandwiches and drinks that have been delivered to the studio, she's also supporting me. Both with my family this morning and during the call, and I appreciate it more than I can say. She didn't sign up for his mess, and if she runs, I won't blame her.

"We'll all get through it together," Axel says at last, breaking into my negative thoughts.

Considering the warning my drummer has given regarding his sister, I'm impressed with Axel's attitude toward him.

"It's going to blow over," the man continues. "Like Naomi said, twenty-four-hour news cycle and all that. Someone else will do something stupid and those idiots outside will move along and bother someone else."

I hope he was right. "Either way, I think the interview is a good move for me. Anyone have any objections to me sitting down alone and digging into my past?" We usually do interviews as a group, and though I often direct the conversation, we're a unit and I respect that.

"You do your thing. Personally, I don't think you owe anybody shit, so if you want to sit on your ass or twiddle your thumbs, go for it. The band's music will ultimately be what matters. But if you want to tell your side and get it off your chest, I respect that, too." Mac says, as he plucks at the strings on his bass guitar, outlining the notes of a recognizable chord.

Axel picks up the rhythm with his sticks and that's that. Another reason I love these guys. For the rest of the afternoon, I lose myself in what I love most, making music.

★ ★ ★

Cassidy

MIDWEEK, I SIT beside Dash in the back of a limousine headed to midtown Manhattan. Naomi has set up his sit-down with a well-known morning show host to give him prime coverage in exchange for an exclusive story. In the days following the blowup at the rehab center, I haven't seen much of him. He's spent most of his time sequestered with the guys in his home recording studio, and I've been busy doing my job.

I've begun meeting with personal assistants who can handle the band's day-to-day needs, be a legitimate assistant and not someone looking for an in with rock stars, and someone who can handle the guys at their fussiest. I've interviewed five people, narrowed it down to two, and scheduled them to return individually early next week to meet the band.

Nights are for the two of us. Neither of us mention the future, and because he deserves the space to get through this emotional upheaval in his life, I keep quiet about it as well. It's clear by the way he tosses and turns and often stares into space, he's stressed about the interview.

I glance to my side. Sunglasses on, he stares out the window, giving me a chance to look him over. He wears a pair of black faded jeans, a white dress shirt, unbuttoned enough to show off his tanned chest and its dusting of hair. He's rolled the shirt at the sleeves, as usual, showing off his sexy tattoos. He has on a pair of black Chucks, and one foot taps like a metronome against the car floor. A black braided-leather necklace enhances his appeal. Add in the sincerity he's sure to bring to the interview and the audience will love him.

I don't think he needs me there when he reveals his past, but the fact that he wants me backstage, *so he can see me when he speaks*, as he'd said when he asked me, touches my heart. That same heart I'm trying to protect.

Yet here I am, my hand on his, as the car pulls up to the back entrance of the studio. A crowd stands outside, and Dash stops to sign autographs, take pictures with his fans, sign a woman's arm, and to my shock, decline a boob sign. I grin at that, quite pleased when he looks at *me*, winked, and returns to the fans. The woman leaves disappointed, but I'm on cloud nine.

The greenroom is well lit, with sofas against the walls, carpet on the floor, and food on a center table, including soft drinks and coffee. As the time slowly ticks by for Dash to go live, he paces the floor in constant motion. Since I can't help him, I sit and watch the show on the screen.

A makeup artist comes in and takes care of evening out his skin tone and getting rid of shine, something I'm used to seeing on set with Sasha and her co-stars.

Then a producer arrives and sets up Dash with his mic. "Ready? Let's get you prepared to walk on set."

"Cass?" Dash holds out his hand.

The producer shakes her head. "She can wait in here."

"No, she can wait in the wings where I can see her." Dash continues to extend his hand. The prima donna rock star side of him that rarely comes out isn't taking no for an answer.

"Fine," the impatient woman mutters. "Let's *go.*" She taps at the Apple Watch on her wrist.

I jump up and grab his clammy hand, holding it for the walk to the studio where the morning show hosts are joking live on camera.

With hand gestures and her finger over her lips, the producer relays directions to me. *Stand here and be quiet.* I get it.

Dash settles himself in a chair beneath heavy lighting, and as soon as the hosts cut to commercial, the female co-host joins in the empty seat across from him. A welcoming smile is on her face and I relax. There's no way this woman is going to skewer him.

They go live and she launches into her introduction, mentioning the band and their success and listing Dash and the guys' accolades. She sobers as she changes the subject to the recent revelations, the rehab confrontation, and then asks Dash for his story.

My palms grow sweaty as I listen to him talk about how, from the time he was a kid, music has been his life, how he and his friend had begun to experiment with drugs, mostly weed until that fateful night, never thinking anything could go wrong. He tells the story about Billy's death, leaving out any mention of his father paying the family for their silence. Bringing that up now would only upset Heather more, and since she hasn't discussed it with the press, we;ve decided this is Dash's story. Not his father's.

His remorse is real and genuine, the raw pain in his voice and expression heart-wrenching. I might be biased when it comes to Dash Kingston, but I have a feeling America will understand his teenage actions.

The show goes to commercial. Dash has one more segment and remains in his seat. I walk to a private corner to quickly check my phone for messages. Axel has texted to check in. I shoot my brother a quick reply to let him know everything is going okay.

The break is long, so I pull up my Instagram account and scroll through, my thumb stopping the screen on a picture Adam has posted. I never deleted or blocked him because he isn't a frequent poster, and in truth, I rarely think about him enough to consider it.

Until now.

The photos, actually a set of photos once I swipe left, stand out. They're staged and set on a gorgeous beach. The first one is a picture of Adam on one knee, an open ring box in hand. A brunette stands in front of him, her eyes wide, her hands over her mouth in *surprise*. I flip to the next picture, which shows the woman's hand, an engagement ring on her finger, a round diamond sparkling in the sunlight. And the final photo displays the happy couple, Adam's fiancée's hand turned out, showing off the ring with the caption, *We're Engaged!* added on to the picture.

I suck in a breath, a combination of shock and nausea hitting me. Not over my ex getting married, I truly have no feelings for him now, but at how quickly he's moved on to this stage of a new relationship.

Have I fallen for Dash? Yes, I have. But while I still have her internal struggle over potential issues between us, Adam has jumped to *getting married*. Which brings up the question, how long have they been seeing each other? Adam and I only broke up a short time ago. Had Adam and his fiancée been sneaking around while I was traveling with Sasha?

I press a hand to my stomach and look around, remembering where I am and realizing I've missed the return to live TV. I rush back to my spot off-stage where Dash can see me. His jaw is tight as he speaks, his tension obvious until he sees me and relaxes back into his seat.

The interview ends shortly afterwards, and I blow out a relieved breath that it's over.

Dash stands and waits while someone removes his microphone, then heads toward me, and I meet him off-stage. Together we walk back to the greenroom.

Nobody else is there and I pull him into a hug. "Good job," I say softly.

"What is it they say? The truth will set you free? Or give the world a story to talk about," he mutters.

I step back and clasp his forearms, the muscles firm beneath my fingers. "You accomplished what you wanted to. You told your side and stopped hiding your pain. Do you feel any better for doing it?" I ask.

"Not as much as I thought I would, which tells me I *need* to talk to Heather."

I nod. "And I understand but it won't be easy."

"But it's necessary."

And I respect his need to do it. "I'm proud of you," I say, my lips meeting his. I care so much for this man, and the thought that what we have now might not last puts a knot in my stomach.

"You can't buy that kind of positive publicity," a familiar voice says, interrupting the kiss.

We break apart, turning at the sound of Dean's voice. I hadn't heard anyone come in. Obviously Dash hadn't either, but Dean stands inside.

"What are you doing here?" Dash asks.

Dean shuts the door behind him and strides over to where we stand. "I'm your manager. It's my job to know where you are and be by your side when you need me."

"Let me guess," Dash says. "You avoided my calls because you didn't want a one-on-one conversation where I could rip you a new one. But you figured if you showed up here, I'd be forced to be nice and not make a scene."

The manager shrugs. "I was giving you time to cool off." Dean, dressed in a suit for his trip to a national morning show, keeps his voice low. "We've had disagreements before about how to handle the little things, and in the end, we worked it out and moved on with what was best for the band. No reason we can't do that again."

"What is best for the band?" Dash's entire body vibrates with anger and his words send chills along my skin. His fury simmers just below the surface, his hands in fists, his jaw set, but Dean is too arrogant to realize how much trouble he's in.

Dean slides his hands into his pockets, lifting his jacket in a slick, contrived move of nonchalance. "Of course. Isn't that my goal? To get you the best deals? To take care of you all?"

I don't buy the man's calm posturing. He knows

he crossed a line by the voicemail Dash left the day of the rehab event and on the messages sent at other times as Dash tried to reach him.

"I don't know, Dean." Obviously agitated, Dash taps a foot on the floor. "How is second-guessing what the band wants in our best interests? How is you treating my girlfriend like dirt a good managerial move? And in what world is you reporting my private visits at an *anonymous* rehab center *taking care* of me?" he asks, voice rising.

I have never heard that low, seething anger in Dash's tone before. He's always been the easygoing brother. The one who laughs most and loudest.

Without thinking, I place a hand on his back, as much to steady him as to let him know he isn't alone.

Dean's gaze locks on the motion, a sneer crossing his face before he catches himself and clears his expression. "Dash, I didn't tell anyone about the meet, but you have to admit the publicity would have been great…had *that woman* not followed you outside hurling accusations," he says of Heather.

Dash shakes his head in obvious disgust. "And there it is. Publicity. That's all that matters to you, isn't it?"

"Of course not!"

"Well, *that woman* lost her brother," he spits out.

I don't know what to say or do to calm him down.

This confrontation needs to happen, and it isn't my place to get in the middle. Even if we *are* in the visitors' room of a television studio.

"It's not enough for you that the Original Kings are a household name," Dash says. "Not enough that we lost Dom and are still on schedule with Axel joining us. Not enough that you've made a fortune on us over the years. You still want *more*, and you don't care at whose or at what expense that comes."

A red stain rises to Dean's cheeks. "That's bullshit and you know it. I'm the voice of reason for the band."

"Reason. Right. First you try and undercut Axel with one of your pet projects, trying to put more money in your pocket by convincing us to take on your drummer of choice. You object to my publicist's idea of Cassidy as the girl on my arm when, let's face it, picking her"—Dash gestures to me—"a woman who is both gorgeous and down-to-earth, makes me look smart and like a changed man. And I don't believe for one minute you didn't call the paps and violate my privacy. So let's just end this now." He folds his arms across his chest and meets Dean's gaze. *"You're fired."*

The manager's eyes open wide, as does his mouth. He clearly never saw this coming. How, I don't know.

Pulling himself together, Dean adjusts his suit

jacket and meet Dash's glare. "You don't want to do that. You *need* me."

Dash raises an eyebrow. "The band believes you're no longer a good fit. We took a vote and it was unanimous. Make no mistake, Dean. This is a group decision." He grasps my hand, clearly ready to walk away.

"This is your fault." Dean points a finger at me, way too close to my chest.

I flinch and take a step back at the same time Dash grabs the digit in his fist. "Don't touch her. Don't make it worse. Just walk away and you'll be hearing from our attorney to finalize things legally."

He releases his hold, and the other man shakes out his hand, a grim, pissed-off expression on his face. "You'd be nothing without me!"

Dash frowns. "Don't mistake my gratitude for the past with my anger now. It's time," he mutters. "Let's go, Cass."

He puts a palm on my back and leads me out of the room, leaving his ex-manager behind.

Dash

I STEP OUTSIDE, the cool fall air settling around me. I

breathe in deep, feeling lighter than I have in ages.

I lead a silent Cassidy to the waiting limo and we climb inside. Leaning back against the seat, I let out a relieved whoosh of air. The interview, smooth as it was, helped my mood somewhat, but firing Dean has lifted the cloud hanging over my head even more. The move was necessary and something that had been building long before Cassidy and I became a couple.

Though Dean blames Cass, the fact is, he and the band outgrew each other long ago. It had just been easier to maintain the status quo rather than deal with firing the man who had given us a chance when nobody else would. Looking back, I wish we'd acted sooner so our parting wouldn't have been so ugly.

I envision more for the Original Kings than we're doing now. Big streaming events and ideas percolate in the back of my head that do not require a manager in order to succeed. With the cache we have in the business, doors will open without one. Bruno Mars, among other artists, ditched his manager years ago and has been reaping the benefits ever since. The Original Kings don't need someone who is more of a liability than an asset taking a cut. No need to replace Dean with another albatross, I think, and plan to sit down with the guys to discuss our future.

I pull out my phone and shoot off a quick note to the guys and our attorney, giving them all a heads-up about me letting Dean go and asking our lawyer to make the termination official and handle any fallout.

With business taken care of, I turn to Cassidy, who I now realize has been uncharacteristically quiet. "Hey. What's up?"

She turns the cell she's been looking at facedown on her lap. "Nothing. I was just letting you take care of business."

"Well, it's all handled for now. What do you say we take the day off and do something fun?"

I'll figure out where and when I want to approach Heather for our talk later. I need to get my thoughts together before I handle that emotional minefield, and a day with Cassidy will help me relax after that interview.

"Don't you need to get back to the studio?" she asks.

"I think we earned a day of playing hooky." Reaching over, I tuck a strand of hair behind her ear. I was a nervous wreck before and during the interview, but looking out and seeing her in the wings settled me every time.

Which reminds me. "Was everything okay earlier? I looked over and didn't see you at the beginning of the second segment."

A look I can't interpret crosses her pretty face. "I was checking in with Axel, and I lost track of time. I didn't mean to be late getting back. But you didn't need me there. You really held your own."

"I disagree. I did need you."

Her eyes glaze over, and she turns to glance out the window, giving me the distinct impression she disagrees.

CHAPTER ELEVEN

Dash

CASSIDY MIGHT BE in a funk that I don't understand, but I'm not going to let her give in to whatever is bothering her. Leaning over, I place a hand on her leg. My attention causes her to turn around and look at me questioningly.

I press a kiss to her cheek. "So … are we taking the day off?" I pick up the question I asked her a few seconds ago.

She shrugs. "What did you have in mind?"

"Just tell me you're in and I'll arrange everything." I want to see a big smile on her face and I know exactly how to accomplish it.

Besides, I'm in the mood to take in the glory of New York City while enjoying the freedom I've begun to feel with her by my side.

Except she still hasn't answered me.

"Is something wrong?" I ask, feeling like I'm repeating a different form of the same question I've already asked her.

She's seemed *off* since I started paying attention to

anything beyond my own drama. I've seen that uncomfortable expression on her face once before, at my family gathering, after Aurora mentioned the naked groupies, but I can't draw a correlation now. She'd laughed off the woman who asked me to sign her boobs and seemed to have been pleased by my response. If something has changed, I'm in the dark.

"No, of course not." She shakes her head too hard and I don't believe her.

I have no choice but to coax her out of her mood and hope she fills me in later. "Good. So let's have some fun."

Picking up my cell, I hit the auto dial for my brother-in-law, a term I'm still getting used to.

"Hi, Beck. Remember the new place in Midtown your developer friend opened recently?" I'm not about to give names and blow the surprise for Cassidy. "Can you get me and Cassidy in today? And give us about a half hour alone once we're there."

"You're kidding," Beck says. "You want me to get an entire exhibit emptied out on your whim?"

I laugh. "Yeah, I know it's a big ask, but you are married to my sister so…"

Cassidy rolls her eyes at my pushiness, and I love the way she handles me. Not kissing my ass. I wink at her and she blushes. Another thing I can't resist. How real she is.

"Rock stars," Beck mutters. "I'll handle it and text you with the details."

"Thanks, man. I mean it," I say to Beck. "I owe you one. Please let them know I'll be giving large donations to the charities their ticket sales support," I say, disconnecting the call.

"What are you up to?" Cassidy asks, a curious expression on her face.

I don't answer. Instead, I tap on the limo partition and speak into the microphone to the driver. "One Vanderbilt," I say.

She narrows her gaze, obviously wondering if we're really going where she thinks, and processing that I've just asked for a brand-new exhibit to be emptied out. If I'd planned ahead, I'd have blindfolded her for the experience, but I'll settle for surprising her the best I can.

I grasp her hand until Beck texts with the name of the man I am to meet and I reply, thanking my brother-in-law again. Since we're already close to the location, when we pull up to the building and the car comes to a stop, I ask the driver to idle for a while. I want to give the manager time to empty out the upstairs for us.

"Are we really going to the SUMMIT?" she asks. "One Vanderbilt Observation Deck?" Cassidy's excitement is finally palpable and she bounces in her seat.

"Yep. There are perks to fame and I want to share them with you."

She grins, placing her hands on my cheeks and planting a thank-you kiss on my lips. Finally, I figure enough time has passed, and I tap on the partition, indicating the driver should let us out.

We exit the car and walk inside, where I meet up with Arthur Golding, the manager, who shakes my hand, then gushes appropriately. I thank him and introduce him to Cassidy. I sign an autograph for the man's granddaughter and make sure to express my gratitude for putting him through the hassle of giving us a private tour with no notice. Somehow Arthur seems to take everything in stride, and I assume it's the charitable donation that softens his mood.

"As arranged by Mr. Daniels, I'm to bring you to the exhibit floors and you have thirty minutes with no one to bother you during your viewing," Arthur says.

"We appreciate it." I squeeze Cassidy's hand.

"You'll need to leave your heels at the entrance," Arthur says. "Normally we ask you to wear soft shoes but … we're making an exception. We just need to protect the floors."

"Of course," Cassidy says. "That's no problem."

"Do you both have sunglasses?" Arthur asks.

"Yes," we both reply.

He nods. "Great. Then we're all set. Follow me to

the elevator, please." He walks away.

Cassidy squeezes my hand tighter. "The Air exhibit," she says in awe.

"My gift to you. I know you've been wanting to see it."

I've caught her reading about the trippy feeling of the glass and mirrored floors and windows and overheard her telling Sasha she's dying to go to the exhibit. I just hadn't thought we'd have the opportunity so soon. But spontaneity is the best.

She smiles wide and I want to grasp her face and pull her lips hard against mine, but Arthur has turned and is waiting for us to catch up. We'll have some alone time soon, and I plan on taking advantage.

Following Arthur into a glass elevator named the Ascent, we ride twelve hundred feet up along the exterior of the building. As our guide explains, we're going to the top three floors of the fourth highest building in the city.

"The artist, Kenzo Digital, created the exhibit with a dreamlike quality, allowing visitors to feel like they are escaping reality. The glass and mirrors will give you quite the experience," Arthur continues to narrate. "And the fact that you are at the highest vantage point in midtown Manhattan will let you look down and see all the reflections of the buildings below."

My stomach flips during the ascent. "Are you

okay?" I ask Cassidy.

She nods, eyes wide, taking in the city below.

The elevator stops, the doors open, and Arthur steps out, gesturing for us to join him.

"I'll be back in half an hour. It won't be enough time for you to see everything, but you will get a taste of the immersive experience. Enjoy!" He steps back into the elevator he's been holding open and leaves us alone on the floor where Air awaits.

Prior to Cassidy, I'll admit I was all about myself. My enjoyment. My pleasure. Women came and went and I never gave them a lingering thought. I knew the moment I laid eyes on her that I'd been sucker-punched for the first time. Everything about her drew me in and still does, from her looks to her laughter, those jade-green eyes, and her loyalty to her best friend.

The night we met, she'd been mistaken for Sasha by a stalker, tasered and attacked in a botched kidnapping attempt. I hadn't acted like myself. I've never been so panicked about a virtual stranger. I've never been so drawn to a woman or as worried about her welfare. To this day, I want to put a smile on her face and keep it there. And I have no idea if she feels the same way.

Which means I am so fucked if she still has those walls a mile high. There are times she is open with me and others when I sense she's hiding, both from me and her own inner pain. Although I have more of my life to repair before I let go of my own burdens, that hasn't stopped my feelings for her from growing beyond my expectations. I'm flying without a safety net if she doesn't reciprocate my feelings.

★   ★   ★

Cassidy

THERE IS NO describing the incredible experience that is SUMMIT One Vanderbilt and the Air exhibit. The day is beautiful, the sky crystal clear, allowing for expansive views of the east side of Manhattan. I'm already light-headed from the physical and dimensional mind manipulation of the exhibit, courtesy of the mirrored and glass views surrounding us, on the floor, the walls, and the ceiling. Though I want to step out onto Levitation, the transparent boxes that protrude from the side of the building, I'm already disoriented, and the vertigo I feel won't allow me to be that brave.

But the entire thirty minutes of wandering the exhibit and staring out at the skyline with Dash by my side has been utterly transcendent. I've kept an eye on the time, wanting to take in as much as I can before Arthur returns for us and the exhibit reopens to the public.

Standing by a floor-to-ceiling window, I turn to Dash, overwhelmed that he listened when I mentioned wanting to see this exhibit. The tickets have been long sold out, and I never thought I'd be able to come.

Yet here we are, and in the midst of his personal drama. "Thank you. I don't know how to express how much this means to me." I look at his sculpted jaw, his dancing blue eyes, and the pleasure on his handsome face. God, he's stunning.

"I'm glad you're enjoying it. It's been incredible to see." He backs me against the glass, his hands on the windows, blocking me in.

His gaze darkens as he steps closer, his lower body flush with mine. His cock is hard and he rubs up against me, letting me know just what I do to him. Desire rushes through me and my panties grow damp. It's safe to say he does the same thing to me.

"Arthur is going to be back any minute," I say in a husky voice I barely recognize.

"I know. And there are probably security cameras around somewhere, so we won't be able to fuck high above the city skyline and give new meaning to the Mile-High Club," he says, clearly disappointed.

My lips twitch in amusement but my pussy clench-es, empty and equally unsatisfied.

Dipping his head, he captures my lips with his and

treats me to a deep, tongue-tangling kiss, leaving no doubt in my mind what he wants before coming up for air. God, I want him, too.

I entwine my arms around his neck, meeting his gaze. "Nobody's ever done something like this for me before. I mean, spur of the moment, you had a sold-out exhibit shut down so we could spend time here." There are perks of being famous and then there's *this*.

He rubs his nose against mine. "If I can't use my rock star status to make you happy, what good is it?"

I blink and suck in a breath. "You mean that, don't you?"

"Of course I do."

Speechless, I'm at a loss. Every emotion I've been holding back comes rushing through me at once, as dizzying as the exhibit around us. *I love this man.*

I love him. I admire his generosity, his depth of feelings for those he cares about, and even his failings and desperation to fix the wrongs in his life. I adore watching him sing and getting lost in his music. And I love the way he lives his life, so free yet so aware that he has an abundance and needs to give back.

I've fallen deeply in love with Dash Kingston.

Unaware of my sudden revelation of feelings, he steps back and adjusts himself, causing me to smile despite the thoughts rushing through my mind.

"Why don't you take some more pictures before

Arthur comes back? I wouldn't want you to miss out on having the memories for posterity."

I can't catch my breath, but he's given me something else to concentrate on, and I latch on to it like a lifeline. "Come here for some photos then."

He turns and stands next to me, our backs to the windows, his arm around my body, smiling, kissing my cheek, and laughing as I snap a couple of selfies with the clouds and the entire cityscape behind us.

We finally make our way back to the limo, both exhausted and exhilarated at the same time. I lay my head on his shoulder and end up dozing on the way back to the Hamptons. He drops me off at my house because he needs to meet with the band and fill them in on the details of his firing Dean. And I'm happy for the time alone to process my thoughts and emotions.

Later that night, alone in bed, I pick up my cell and begin to scroll through the myriad photos I took earlier today. The sheer fun and joy of the afternoon comes rushing back along with the look in Dash's eyes as he'd bracketed me against the glass overlooking the city, and my stomach twists with profound need.

And then I remember the Instagram engagement photos of Adam and his fiancée. Though I can't deny how well Dash treats me or how he looks at me like I mean everything to him, my stomach still churns with worry. It isn't just the fact that he'll go on tour one day and be exposed to all the vices that come along with his status. It's my past that keeps me in a near constant state of upheaval, too.

How the hell could Adam dump me by text after four years together? Is my radar that off where relationships are concerned? Had he been cheating on me while I traveled for work? And does that mean I shouldn't trust my judgment … or Dash?

I shake my head, annoyed I could be so distrustful of a man who's done everything to show me I'm important to him.

No, I think, I can't lump Dash in with Adam. I need to give him the benefit of the doubt because clearly he has strong feelings for me.

And God knows, I've fallen hard for him.

THE NEXT MORNING, I realize Dash never came to my house last night. A glance at my phone tells me he'd texted after I fell asleep. He and the guys had started to play, and they were on to something with a song. He told me he was working through the night and has plans to go see Heather this morning. I wince on reading that, hoping he'll be okay. He also told me to take the day off and promised to be in touch later on.

I smile, glad the music is flowing for him and

equally worried about his talk with Billy's sister. I admire the strength it takes for him to face the woman after the scene she'd made last weekend.

After a shower, I sit with a cup of coffee and scroll through the news on my cell. The phone in my hand rings, startling me. I don't recognize the number, but something makes me answer anyway.

"Hello?"

"Hi, is this Cassidy Forrester?" a somewhat familiar female voice asks.

"Yes? How can I help you?"

"Hi, Cassidy, it's Joanne, Russell Wilson's secretary."

"Joanne! How are you?" When I worked at the ad agency in LA before meeting Sasha, Russell Wilson, the senior vice president of Fundamental Documentaries, had been a client. Joanne and I had talked often on the phone.

"I'm great! You?"

I smile. "Same. So what are you doing reaching out?"

"Well, Russell moved to Netflix three months ago and took me with him," Joanne says.

"Oh, wow! I hadn't heard." Then again I've been immersed in Sasha's world, then moved to the Original Kings and music. "Congratulations! That's a big jump."

"Thank you. Russell would like to talk to you about a position on his team at Netflix. He's working in the Original Content Division."

"Oh, wow." My heart begins pounding in my chest. "Are you serious?"

Joanne laughs. "Would I be calling otherwise? He's thinking you would make a wonderful creative director."

My hands begin to tremble, but I steady myself and take a deep breath. Once I've pulled myself together, I clear my throat and assume a more professional tone.

"That's very exciting. When would he like to talk?" I have no desire to live in Los Angeles again, where Netflix is located, when my family and friends are in New York, but Netflix is a huge opportunity. One I would be a fool not to at least consider.

"He'd like you to fly out and meet with him and other people on his team."

My mouth grows dry. "I appreciate the opportunity. Can I get back to you?"

"Of course, but soon, okay? He has a short list but you're at the top."

"Yes. I will be in touch soon. Thanks, Joanne. It's great to hear from you." I disconnect the call and stare at the screen, which has gone from the call back to the photos I'd been scrolling through.

Photos of me and Dash.

What will he say when I tell him I've been offered a job in LA for the world's leading streaming service? What would Sasha think? I've committed to Sasha and her company, yet I have no doubt my friend would encourage me to explore such a huge opportunity. And Dash hasn't made me any promises. That scares me most of all.

★ ★ ★

Dash

I FINALLY RETURN home from a long session with the guys that has me high on our collaboration. At some point I'll crash hard from lack of sleep, but right now I'm still fueled by adrenaline. Nothing is better than a jam session that results in new music. I can't wait to share the news with Cassidy. I know how happy she'll be to find out how well her brother gels with the band.

But I gave her the day off so I can take care of personal business. Meeting with Billy's sister is something I have to do alone. Until I put my one-to-one talk with Heather behind me, I can't move forward the way I want to.

I call the rehab center and ask to speak to Heather, and when she picks up, I ask if I can stop by later today, on one of her breaks. And though she doesn't really want to see me, I somehow convince her to let me come.

I jump into the shower, dry off, dress, grab my keys, and head out. Heart pounding in my chest, I pull up to the center. The parking lot is fairly empty, which helps my nerves. No repeat of the other day. Then again, nobody who would snitch knows where I am.

I cut the engine of my Ferrari and head inside. I ask the woman manning the front desk to call for Heather, and then I wait for her to join me.

She strides down the hall with a frown on her face, the same expression she displays every time we're in close proximity to one another.

She steps up to me, eyebrows raised, as if to say, *Now what?*

I sigh and glance outside. "It's a nice day. How about we take a walk." At least then we'll have privacy.

"Whatever gets this over with faster," she says, storming past me and heading out the door before I can step forward and hold it open for her.

"Great," I mutter, following her out and catching up with her halfway down the sidewalk. "Heather, please stop."

She turns to face me, arms folded across her chest. "Why do we have to do this?"

I groan and run my hand through my hair. "Because we both need to have our say in private." I gesture toward her with one hand. "Go ahead. Tell me off. Yell about how much you hate me, how I should be dead and your brother should be here. How it's all my fault."

"It's not your fault, it's mine! I should have been home that night," she says, tears in her eyes.

I blink, stunned by the admission and immediately knowing how wrong she is. "We were seventeen. Old enough to be home alone."

Heather was two years older, and the few times she'd come into the garage to listen to us play, I recall her complaining about how cold it was before leaving us alone.

"Even if you had been there, you wouldn't have been in the garage with us. Heather, it wasn't your fault." Though I want to reach out and touch her, to comfort her in some small way, I know it wouldn't be welcome.

"*You* bought the drugs, right?" Her glassy eyes meet mine.

I shove my hands into my pockets and force myself to meet her gaze. To own what I've done. "I did."

And though I want to make excuses, to explain it was the first time we planned to try coke, that I had no way of knowing the stuff had been laced, I clench my jaw and say nothing more.

"I remember your father coming over the morning after. He and my parents talked in the kitchen." She rubs at her already red nose. "I heard your father say that Billy bought the coke but I knew … Billy didn't have the money for cocaine. And he once told me he was afraid to go to that part of town."

All I can do is stand and wait for her to continue and listen.

"My parents believed your father because he had money. They were in awe of him. And when he offered them a check, you have no idea how much it eased their financial burden."

So she *did* know about the money. Makes sense, given she was the older sibling.

She swallows hard. "They believed your father because it made their lives easier, but the story never rang true to me."

I let out a snort. "That's because you were right. You have good instincts." I dip my head. "I am so damned sorry, Heather. It won't bring Billy back any more than the money did, but I needed you to know. And that's why I did the interview yesterday. To take the responsibility now because I couldn't when I was seventeen."

"Because you were in awe of your dad, too?" she asks.

I shake my head. "Because nobody said no to

Kenneth Kingston. Especially his kids." I groan. "Look, I can't fix what I did but I need you to know that I'm sorry. And I hope…" I shake my head. "Never mind. Just be well."

I turn and start for the parking lot, to the safety of my car. And when I climb inside and start the engine, I grip the wheel and exhale a long breath. She hasn't forgiven me, but that isn't why I came. I needed to own my mistakes and apologize. What Heather does with that information, whether it brings her any peace, I'll never know. But I hope with everything in me she can let go of her anger and live a happy life.

I feel lighter, like a burden has been lifted from my shoulders now that the secret I've kept has come to light and I've faced down my past.

The spot in front of me is empty, with no barrier blocking my way. I shift and tear out of the parking lot, hitting the main road and breathing for the first time since entering the facility. And though I haven't yet slept and am exhausted, I still have one more important thing to do today.

One that will define the rest of my life. I can crash and sleep later.

I pull into the driveway of my house and head inside, finding it empty. The guys are probably in their rooms, out cold. I stop in the kitchen to get a bottle of water, open it, and chug half the cold liquid, placing it on the counter.

My doorbell rings, surprising me. I walk to the door and glance out the side window to see Cassidy standing on the porch. Happy to see her, I open the door and greet her with a smile. One she returns but those clouds are still in her eyes. Eyes the color of a rolling field of grass.

She wears a light coating of makeup on her pretty face. Her hair falls around her shoulders, and my fingers itch to tangle in the long strands and tug while I make love to her. And there's that word. The one I haven't let fully form in my head … and yet it has made itself known anyway.

Shit. My stomach churns in panic. Ironically, not because of my feelings. She's saved me a trip to her house to tell her … but she doesn't look like a woman ready to hear my declaration. And I've never said it before to anyone outside of my family. The thought of baring my soul and having her freak out isn't part of my plan. Not that I have much of one to begin with.

"Come on in," I say.

She steps into the house and I shut the door behind her. "Good night in the studio?" she asks.

"The best. When I say we gelled…" I shake my head, that high from earlier this morning returning. "It was one of those times where everything fell into place. I can just feel how good this album is going to be."

A genuine smile graces her lips. "I am so happy to hear that. I'm thrilled. For all of you."

"Thanks. Me too." I gesture for her to come inside, and she follows me to the family room. Though I want to tell her about Heather, whatever is on her mind is much more important. "Okay, talk to me," I say, as we settle onto the big, comfy couch.

"About what?" she asks.

"Whatever's going on in that head of yours. I can feel the tension coming from you a mile away."

She blows out a long stream of air and nods. "Okay. Yes, I have something to tell you."

That's never a good start to any conversation, and suddenly my stomach is in total knots.

"I got a call from someone I used to work with when I was at an ad agency, prior to becoming Sasha's personal assistant," she says.

I wait because obviously that isn't everything.

She twists her hands together in front of her, her own nerves showing. "He used to work for a documentary company and recently took another job. And he'd like to offer me a position on his team. At Netflix. Or I should say he'd like me to come out and meet his team, and if things go well, he'll make a formal offer."

I blink at her news, unsure what that means for

Sasha, but Netflix is huge, and Cassidy deserves any break that comes her way. "That's exciting!" I say, supporting her all the way.

"It's in LA."

My thoughts stop cold. Not to mention my heart. "What?"

Those big eyes met mine. "Netflix is located in LA." She bites down on her lower lip, and for the first time, I have no sexual reaction. Not when my emotions are in a tailspin.

I've spent the last month showing Cassidy I'm not just a changed man but the man for her. And now, as I plan to use the *L* word, she's talking about moving across the country. Or is she?

"Well? What do you think?" she asks.

I think I want you to say fuck the job and stay. But how can I say that when she's looking at a potential career changer with a company that could open all sorts of doors for her in the future?

I draw a steadying breath. "What kind of job?"

"Creative director. The same as the position with Sasha, Xander, and Harrison," she says, her hands still twisted into knots.

But with *Netflix.* Neither one of us needs to repeat the name.

"It's their Original Content Division," she adds. "I haven't done any research yet. I'm in shock, you know?"

"Yeah. I know." So am I.

"Dash, you didn't answer me. What do you think about it?" she asks.

Oh, no. I'm not going to make a decision for her. "More importantly, what do *you* think about it?"

She bites her lip. Again. "I don't know. On the one hand, I've committed to Sasha already. On the other, it's a huge opportunity."

I nod, noticing she hasn't mentioned me. I force out my next words. "I agree."

"And maybe I owe it to myself to hear them out?" She sounds tentative yet … Netflix.

Jesus. I run a hand through my hair and glance down. Her poor hands are getting a workout, and I place my palms over her contorted fingers. "I think that's a smart idea. You don't want to look back and have any regrets."

And I don't want her to blame me for a missed opportunity, which she might if I ask her to stay. Even if I do want to get down on my knees and beg, I can't hold her back. For once in my life, I need to be selfless, not selfish.

"I see." She slides her hands from beneath mine. "You don't want me to stay?"

"Of course I do. We're good together, but you need to decide after you've heard what Netflix has to offer. I want you to be happy, Cass. And to follow your dreams."

She blinks, nodding at his words, her face a blank mask. "You're right. I'll talk to Sasha and let her know what's going on." She rises to her feet and I immediately stand, too. "I'm glad we're on the same page," she says softly.

We are so far from being on the same page it isn't funny, I think.

She rushes to the door, and I walk her out, standing on the porch as she waves before climbing into her car. And as she drives away, my stomach feels as if it has been scooped out and dumped in the trash. Doing the right thing has never hurt as badly as it does now, and given the last week, that's saying something.

I love her and I didn't tell her. I encouraged her to go listen to a job offer on the other side of the country, and she readily agreed. Is this karma for my behavior toward women in the past? Is it what I deserve because of what happened with Billy?

I shake my head hard. I didn't even have a chance to tell her about my meeting with Heather. Maybe that's a good thing, since I'm probably going to have to get used to doing things on my own and coming home to an empty house.

And an even emptier bed.

CHAPTER TWELVE

Cassidy

*D*ASH LET ME *go*. He hadn't even attempted to ask me to stay.

I wait until I've turned the corner and am out of sight of his house before pulling over and letting the tears flow. Although I hadn't let myself admit it, I wanted him to ask me to stay. To put us above everything else because he loves me.

There is a voice in my head that asks why I hadn't just told him I loved him. But then I think about his life as a famous rock star who's never had a relationship, has never wanted one, and I can't help but need him to put himself out there first.

I gave him the chance, too. Not just by telling him about the offer but by asking him what his thoughts were about it. He'd thrown the choice back at me, which, of course, makes sense. It's my life, my offer. But I can't help but think, maybe this job offer has made it easier for him in the long run. Just like maybe my travel with Sasha had made it simpler for Adam to find the woman he actually was meant to spend his life with. After all, Adam and I had been together almost four years and he hadn't asked *me* to marry him. Not that I'd wanted to, but that isn't the point.

I draw a deep breath and head to Sasha's to talk to her and let her know I'm going to fly to LA and see what Russell's offer entails. I have no doubt my friend will understand.

As for Dash? I'll chalk it up to yet another disappointing experience with a man—except this one has broken my heart.

★　★　★

Dash

THE NEXT DAY, the band gathers in the studio, excited to pick up where we left off yesterday. Well, Jagger, Mac, and Axel are bouncing and ready to go. I'm in a crappy mood from lack of sleep and losing the woman I love. No, she hasn't officially taken the job, but from the way yesterday's conversation went, I have no idea if, should she decide to stay in New York, she'd be coming back to me.

I feel the itch in my throat and can't decide if I'm coming down with something. Something besides a stupid case of self-pity.

I check my phone. Still no word from Cassidy.

"Let's go again," Jagger says, pacing the studio.

Easier said than done when all you have to do is strum a couple of strings.

"Fine." I chug warm honey and water to ease my scorched vocal cords after a full day of recording.

Of course this has to be the song with the crazy-ass fast lyrics. As I sing them, I mentally pat myself on the back, right before my voice cracks in the middle of a long note.

"That's enough." Mac says, laying down his bass. "We aren't going to get this today."

I hear the judgment in his tone and know I deserve it. "My throat's raw, man. I'll record the track separately. It'll be EQ'd that way anyway," I say, thinking about how our producer likes to work.

"I agree. Let's end this for today." Axel shoves his sticks in his back pocket and strides over to Dash. "You. Outside. We need to talk."

I frown and follow my bandmate into the fresh air. I'm still working on my friendship with the man because things are so new, but I have no complaints with how he fits in with the band.

We end up outside by the now-covered pool, breathing in the cooler fall air. "What the fuck?" Axel asks. "Yesterday you were on fire. Today you can't crap a lyric."

I run a hand through my hair. "I'm preoccupied,"

he mutters.

"No shit."

I kick a stone, and it bounces across the patio.

"I don't like sticking my nose in anyone else's business, but I have to ask. How do you feel about my sister?" Axel asks.

I jerk my head up and meet the man's gaze. No point in denying the truth. "I love her."

Axel blinks, and it isn't from the glare of the sun. "So why the hell did you let her go?"

I have no answer that will satisfy either of us emotionally, but I do have the truth. "I didn't want her to give up such a big opportunity without seeing what it entailed. I didn't want to hold her back, and I sure as hell don't want her to have any regrets if she stays just because I told her how I feel."

Axel shakes his head and groans. "Seriously? I didn't like this relationship in the beginning, but even I can see you two are good for each other."

I consider that the ultimate compliment.

He glances up at the clouds dotting the blue sky and continues. "Like I told you the night after the VMAs, Cassidy isn't the type to deal with her pain. She shuts down instead. Case in point, our parents died when we were young, but when our grandma who raised us passed, Cassidy was sixteen. She didn't fall apart. Instead she fortified her walls, continued to go to school, maintained her grades, but kept her friends at a distance. Second time? Her ex broke up with her over text, it was barely a blip on her radar. *I told you all this.*"

Axel studies me before continuing. "You don't get it, do you?" He shakes his head, clearly as frustrated as I am.

"Just explain it to me, okay?"

"Fine. She came to you, told you about the job offer, and gave you every opportunity to ask her to stay. To tell her how you felt about her. And what did you do? You told her to *go clear across the country* and hear out the offer. To go chase her dreams. Good fucking going, man."

"Of course I did! She deserves everything!"

"But she wants you—not that I have a fucking clue why at this point—and you didn't tell her you felt the same way. Jesus. She'd just found out on Instagram that her ex got engaged, and she assumes he'd been with the woman prior to breaking up with her. You letting her go was the last straw." Axel has begun pacing, his hands curled into fists.

"Whoa. *What?*"

Axel spins around to face me. "Pretty sure you heard me."

Yeah, I had. "She didn't tell me." I pause, then ask, "When did she find out?"

Axel clenches his jaw before speaking. "Earlier in the day. While you were on live television."

And that explains why she'd pulled back after my interview. Fuck. I pull at my hair in frustration. "I didn't know."

"Well, now you do," Axel mutters.

"Did she leave today?"

The other man shrugs. "No idea. I spoke to her yesterday. She was going to be checking into flights. She said they needed to see her out there soon." He eyes me warily. "I have one more thing to say."

"Might as well go for it." I've been beaten over the head so hard I can't feel it anymore.

"I don't know what's going on in your head, but I can tell you one thing for sure. If she gets to LA but ultimately decides to stay in New York, which she will because her family is here, and you haven't stepped up beforehand?"

"She'll think she's nothing but a convenience to me." I wonder if I can rip out my own hair.

"Exactly. She won't trust you when you're on the road, and you two won't stand a chance at making it in the future."

Hearing Cassidy's brother lay it on the line sends me spiraling, but I know enough to realize what I need to do. "She needs a grand gesture," I say.

Axel tips his head to the side. "Maybe you're not as

dumb as you've made yourself out to be. But I still can't believe I had to lead you here like a fucking horse to water."

I let out a laugh. "I caught on awhile back. I just knew you needed to have your say." No need to let Axel get a bigger head thinking he guided me to the right path.

I might have been slow getting to this point, but I'm not going to fuck it up in the end. Now I just have to hope Cassidy isn't already on a plane to California.

★ ★ ★

Cassidy

I REALIZE THE moment I board the plane at JFK International Airport that I've made a mistake. Actually, I accepted my error on the two-hour car ride from East Hampton to the airport. But I'd pushed on, sitting for a few hours at the terminal during a delay. Now, my carry-on—because I'm not planning on staying more than a day or two—is in the plane's overhead compartment. My purse is under the seat and my heart is in my throat.

What am I doing? I don't want to live in Los Angeles alone without my brother or Sasha. Or Dash, but that's another thought process altogether.

If I stay in New York and Dash isn't in love with me and doesn't want a future, I might wish I'd taken the job in California after all. But at least I'd have all the other people in my life surrounding me while I healed. As for my professional future, I know for sure it lies with Sasha's production company.

I'm loyal, and I want to be with K-Talent Productions from the ground up. I want to be by my best friend's side as she builds her company and makes a splash in the industry. And I'm sorry I let my fear and sadness about how Dash had reacted dictate my choices. No matter how encouraging and understanding Sasha has been, I should never have considered this new position when I don't really want it.

I pick up my bag from the floor. Thank goodness I have an aisle seat, I think, as I stand and take my small suitcase from the top compartment. Everyone has already boarded, but the plane doors aren't yet shut, which means I have to get out of here fast, before the small window of opportunity to leave closes. I don't think I can bear five hours on this plane only to end up where I don't want to be, far from home, for no good reason.

I ease my way down the aisle and tell the flight attendant I'm not making the trip. I have to give my name so they can adjust their passenger list and head count, then I walk back down the jet bridge toward the airport gate, at peace with my decision.

I won't regret not flying to LA to find out more about this job, but I would most definitely regret leaving Dash without telling him that I love him. All of my issues with worrying about other women and his past are just that. My issues. Reasons I've used to keep him at a distance because my feelings for him are so big they scare me. Getting on a plane to run away because I didn't have the courage to face my fears or trust in him is stupid.

If he isn't ready for a serious relationship or commitment, if one day we broke up … New York is still where I belong.

And dammit, I want Dash to be my home.

I walk back into the airport and pause to catch my breath. In a few minutes I'll make my way outside and call for a car to take me back to my house. A long two-hour drive, or more if there's traffic.

At least the distance will give me time to plan what to say to Dash.

Dash

I HAVE NEVER been more grateful for my Ferrari than I am on the drive to John F. Kennedy International

Airport, hoping I can catch Cassidy before she leaves for LA. Thank God she'd given Sasha her airline and flight number since she left her brother in the dark. Sasha, bless her loyal soul, didn't want to share the information, but I swore to her that one way or another, I'm bringing Cassidy home. Even if I have to catch a last-minute flight to California to do it.

Without a suitcase or even a fully formed plan, I buy a ticket to LA on the next available flight. Cassidy's flight is sold out, and regardless, I need the boarding pass in order to get past security. I run through the airport, pausing at the flight board, checking the plane's status, and my stomach sinks when I see the word *departed* on the display.

"Shit." I shake my head, walk to the nearest seat, and lower myself into it to catch my breath from my sprint.

Once I can think clearly, I realize I have four hours before the flight I've booked, and wondered if the Kingston company private jet can get me there any faster. Of course, I'd have to make the forty-five minute to an hour car ride to Teterboro, where Linc keeps the plane.

"Son of a bitch." I run a hand through my hair, then pull my cell from the front pocket of my hoodie to call my brother.

"Dash?"

Thinking I'm hallucinating the familiar voice, I keep my gaze on the screen and scroll for Linc's number in my favorites. With such a large family, I have a lot of people listed in there.

"Dash!"

I can't ignore the two feet in a pair of pink Chucks right in front of me, and I lift my gaze. Cassidy stands there staring, a perplexed expression on her face.

I've never been so fucking relieved in all my life. "Cass? Jesus. I thought your flight took off. What happened?"

I jump to my feet, taking in her traveling outfit, a pair of jeans, those pink sneakers, and a white blouse over a black tank top. Her hair is pulled into a ponytail with long strands falling around her makeup-free face, and she's never looked more beautiful.

She tilts her head to one side. "What are you doing here?"

"I asked first." I sound like a fucking child and all but cringe.

"I decided not to go to LA."

I want to ask why, but as she wraps her arms around herself in a defensive gesture, I see firsthand she no longer trusts me. If she ever really did.

She stares at me, obviously waiting for me to explain my presence at the airport. It's time to man up and tell her why I've come. To risk being the one to open my heart first. The same heart beating hard in my chest.

Looking into her eyes, I say, "I was hoping to catch you before you boarded your flight, but I looked at the display and realized your plane had taken off and I was too late."

"You're not too late," she whispers, giving me hope that she means those words in more ways than the obvious one.

I draw a deep breath and pull out the ticket I'd bought. "I'm booked on the next flight to LA in four hours, but I was trying to figure out if Linc's private jet could get me to you faster." I'm rambling but I need her to know the lengths to which I was willing to go to find her.

Her tongue swipes over her bottom lip. Unable to stop myself, I brace my hands on either side of her face and pull her in for a too-brief kiss. "I need you to know that I want to give you the world."

Her gaze softens and her eyes fill with tears. "Then why did you let me go?"

Because I'm an ass. "I didn't want you to have any regrets later, but encouraging you to leave … It broke my heart. As your brother pointed out, you all but told me you wanted to stay, and I was too thick-headed to realize it."

She swallows hard and laughs, no doubt at her

brother's helpful interference. "I was looking for a clue that you didn't want me to take the job, and when I didn't get it, I figured you weren't as invested in us as I was."

She grabs on to my sweatshirt and pulls me toward her. "I shouldn't have booked the flight let alone gotten on the plane when everything I need is in New York."

"Yeah? And what is that?"

She nibbles on her lower lip, and this time I have an extremely sexual reaction. Thank God my sweatshirt is big and nobody is looking at the bulge in my jeans.

"When I was in my seat and trying not to have an anxiety attack, I realized that my family is in New York, that Axel and Sasha are there."

She hasn't mentioned me, but she still holds onto my shirt, which gives me the strength to wait while she explains.

"I thought about the job and realized I wouldn't regret not flying to LA to talk to Russell Wilson but I would regret not telling you that I loved you."

Her grip on my sweatshirt tightens, and at her admission, my heart soars.

She goes on. "I also knew that even if you didn't reciprocate my feelings, getting off the flight was the right thing to do for myself."

Relief rushes through me faster than my baby, the Ferrari, takes a highway. "It was the best thing you could have done for *us*." I brush a strand of hair off her face and tuck it behind her ear, grateful I can touch her again, knowing she's here to stay, and most importantly, she's *mine*.

All hesitancy gone, she smiles wide. "I know. Because you were waiting for me, which means you love me, too."

I laugh. This woman is perfect for me in so many ways. "So not only did you tell me first, you didn't give me a chance to say it back."

"I pretty much thought the fact that you rushed here to stop me from leaving said it all. But I wouldn't mind hearing the words from those talented lips." She traces the outline of said lips with her finger, and I feel the zing of her touch right down to my soul.

"I love you, Cassidy Forrester." And though it's too soon right now, I intend to lock her into an engagement before I leave on my next tour.

Hell, if I have my way, I'll marry her before then, too. I want to give her every reason to trust me while we are apart. A wedding ring, not just on her finger but on mine, too, will go a long way toward getting rid of any lingering insecurities she has thanks to my past. Not to mention the pain of abandonment in hers. We will have each other for the rest of our lives and nothing could make me happier. With luck, she feels the same way. We have time to talk about things in depth when we get home. To truly make sure we're in it for the long haul.

Together.

"Cass?" I ask.

"Hmm?"

"Let's go home."

Cassidy

LET'S GO HOME.

Those words are music to my ears, pun intended. I never expected to see Dash on my way out of the airport, and when I'd laid eyes on his familiar form, I thought I was seeing things. Hearing him say he'd tried to stop me from boarding? The most unexpected, best news ever.

Now that I've come to terms with the fact that my hang-ups have nothing to do with how Dash will behave, my heart is open and my walls are down.

I meet his gaze, smiling wide. "Yes. Let's go home."

He lifts me into his arms, and I wrap my legs around his waist, my body floating in a state of euphoria.

"I love you, Cass," he whispers in my ear and my entire being reacts.

"I love you, too, Dash."

He spins me around, and when he stops, I realize we have an audience of mostly females, phones on, directed toward us, obviously recording our happy reunion.

"Dash! Can I get your autograph?"

"Will you sign my sweatshirt?"

"Dash, can we take a picture?"

Fan after fan shouts out requests, uncaring that he's obviously otherwise occupied. I know I have to get used to this part of his life and sharing him, and there is no time like the present to show him I can handle it.

"You should put me down and greet your fans," I tell him, arms wrapped tightly around his neck so I won't fall.

He shakes his head. "I'm not letting you go. I made that mistake once in this lifetime. I'm not doing it again." He turns to face our audience. "Everyone, this is my girlfriend, who I'm going to marry one day," he announces. "You all can let the world know I said that."

"Dash!" I exclaim, taken off guard by his pronouncement but totally on board.

Female shouts and squeals follow.

"As much as I love you all, today is about us. So no autographs or selfie pics this time. Hope you forgive me."

And then, in front of our audience, he dips his head and kisses me long and hard, to what I realize is the sound of applause.

EPILOGUE

Cassidy

Four Years Later

"**I** HAVE NO business being at this movie premier. Look at me! I'm the size of a whale," I say, my arms barely reaching around my extremely pregnant belly.

Dash shakes his head. "You're the most beautiful woman in the room." Leaning over, he kisses my cheek and I shiver. It never ceases to amaze me how our chemistry never changes. He always affects me and vice versa.

"You have to say that. We're married and I'm not letting you go anywhere. Especially not now that I'm due any minute."

He chuckles and runs his hand over my bare back. "You're the film's producer and Sasha's right hand in the company. You wouldn't miss tonight for anything."

The man has a point. Still, it really isn't fair the way the timing has worked out.

I had come on board as creative director, and I worked my ass off for the first year, proving my worth to my three bosses. On the one-year anniversary of the company's opening, they'd offered me a new position, head of Film and Television. In other words, I became Sasha's right hand, something I'm well used to being. My job was to pick projects for the company and run them by Sasha as well as deal with the day-to-day workings of our various projects.

K-Talent Productions may have started as a film production company, but quickly moved into the television and streaming worlds, too. We are a media company with a collaborative culture, which is perfect for both me and Sasha.

I had found the script for tonight's premiere movie screening and knew immediately we had a hit on our hands. The premise was that a woman who escapes an abusive marriage begins living under a new name and fighting for the life she wants to live versus staying under the radar of her ex. A female regaining her power against the man who tried to keep her down is the kind of story that appealed to me on a deep level, and I knew Sasha would be perfect for the lead female role, Harrison for the lead male.

Sasha hadn't starred in anything since getting back together with Xander. But Harrison had agreed to film in New York if they co-starred together. The compromise worked, both for Sasha's marriage and for Harrison, who was single and flexible. To my shock, Sasha, Xander, and Harrison had asked me to be the film's producer. With Dash touring, I wanted to keep busy, and I threw myself into the job.

I can't believe this is my life. Along with the man beside me, who has super-sperm, because this baby hadn't been planned, but he or she is very wanted. I have it all.

Since I know what it's like to struggle growing up, I also wanted to give back and have joined in running a charity for foster kids who age out of the system and have nowhere to go. The charity was Dash's sister Aurora's idea, because that had been her life experience until the Kingstons found her. Sasha had founded a charity in LA and turned over the running of it to the director, but she had the experience to get things up and running. I took over outreach and fundraising. Considering I often meet famous people I can hit up for donations, I'm perfect for the job.

"Where did you go?" Dash asks me.

I shake my head, clearing out my thoughts. "I was thinking back over the last four years to how much has changed. How I got to this point," I say, glancing around at the people getting ready to head into the theater to watch my movie.

"You got to this point by getting off that plane,"

he reminds me. "Of course, I'd have tracked you down and brought you home anyway." He sounds way too pleased with himself.

"Behave or you're not getting lucky when we get home." Somehow, despite my big belly, we've kept our love life intact.

We're perfect together, blending our lives and managing his career without me losing my mind. I'm proud to say I've handled two tours like a pro.

If you don't count the fact that I fly out to see him whenever I can, which, as the production company grows, becomes less and less. But I trust the man I married.

The band still writes music, but they've put off touring for at least another year, which helps since I don't want to do the first year of this baby's life alone. Dash has discovered he's happiest writing songs, and he's begun doing so for other bands who approach him on collaboration in addition to the Original Kings. Life is good.

"Dash, Cassidy!" Aurora calls our names and walks over to where we're standing. She's grown as a woman and a mother, and I adore my sister-in-law.

"Who's watching the princess?" I ask of Leah, who is now five and thinks she rules the world. With so many aunts and uncles at her beck and call, she actually does.

Aurora pushes her long hair over her bare shoulder. She looks gorgeous in her evening gown. "I have a babysitter who lives in the neighborhood."

Aurora has moved out of Dash's mom's mansion and now lives in a townhouse community nearby. "If Leah doesn't wear her out and she's willing to come back next time I need her, I consider it a win."

Dash laughs. "Maybe she'll play guitar for her all night?" He's referring to the last Christmas present he bought her, for which Aurora has given him hell. Especially after Leah started waking her up at five every morning by playing. Badly. The child does not take after her talented uncle when it comes to music, at least not yet. But she's young and there is time.

"Funny," Aurora mutters. "I cannot wait to see the film!"

"I'm so nervous, I'm not sure if the twisting in my stomach is the baby or anxiety!" I say, rubbing my lower back.

"Babe, you've got this. They're already talking about Oscar and Golden Globe nominations. I'm so proud of you." Dash hugs me to his side.

"Don't remind me," I say, still holding on to my belly.

"Are you feeling okay?" Aurora asks, her face scrunched in concern.

I blow out a breath. "I am. I'm just tired. We made

the rounds when we arrived," I say, referring to how, in my role of producer, I had to stop and talk to everyone who matters who has come tonight. Not to mention the entire Kingston clan and Harrison's family, who'd flown in from all corners of the country.

"And that's why we found a place to hide out in for a little while," Dash says.

Aurora nods. "I remember how tough it was at the end of my pregnancy. You should get off your feet and rest."

"She's right," Dash says, his concern also obvious.

I sigh. "Soon." I glance around and take in the people I haven't yet spoken to. "Looks like Harrison's family is as close as yours." I gesture to the people surrounding him, extremely handsome men whose genes are strong, their resemblance to one another impossible to miss.

"The Dirty Dares," Aurora says with a smile, clearly amused by the name.

"Yes. Their vodka is world famous and extremely good… I wish I could have a drink before I have to sit through an hour and a half of everyone watching the first movie I produced."

"The doctor said you can have a small glass of white wine," Dash reminds me.

"Oh, my God," Aurora says, her voice shaking.

I glance at the woman who looks suddenly pale.

"What's wrong?" Dash immediately clasps his sister's elbow and pulls her toward him.

She shakes her head. "Nothing... I... There's someone who looks familiar but..."

I turn to see one of the Dare men approaching.

"I ... I need the ladies' room," she says and dashes away, leaving us confused.

I turned toward the Dares again only to see the man watching Aurora as she rushes off, a dazed expression on his face. Then he spins in the direction she went.

"Do you know what that was about?" I ask Dash, who is only aware of his sister's hasty retreat, not the man who's gone after her.

Dash shakes his head. "Not a clue but she looked like she saw a ghost."

"I should go check on her," I murmur, only to be stopped by a horrendous cramp. "Oh!" I double over, nearly falling against Dash as I grab my belly.

"What is it?" Dash grasps my shoulders and meets my gaze. "Babe, talk to me."

I blink, the pain subsiding. "Nothing ... I was just..." It feels like a bubble bursts inside me, and water begins trickling down my legs. "Oh, no. No, no, no. Not now!"

"Cass?"

"My water broke!" I moan.

"Looks like you won't have to sit around for an hour and a half while all these people watch the first movie you've produced." Dash means it as a joke, but the fear in his eyes and on his face is real.

"Hey, guys." Axel strides up to us, a drink in his hand. "How's it going?"

I step back. The hem of my gown is wet, and a puddle of water sits on the floor while stuff still trickles down my legs. "My water broke," I whisper.

Axel's mouth opens wide. He glances from me to Dash, who has frozen in place.

"Hey, Dash!" Axel's voice rises above the din. "Now's not the time to panic." He shakes my husband by the shoulders. "You hear me?"

Dash nods. "I'm fine. Sorry. I'm good."

I roll my eyes. "You'd think he was having the baby."

"What did you say about having a baby?" Jordan asks as she pulls Linc into our tight circle.

"My water broke. I need to get to the hospital without calling attention to myself. I don't want to ruin this night for Sasha or Harrison."

I know this family, and they'll drop everything, including the premiere of a movie they star in, to come to the hospital to see their niece or nephew being born. And I don't want Dash's mom to feel torn between her son and her daughter.

"Come on. Can you walk out of here?" Dash, his arm now around me, asks.

"If I don't… Shit!" I bend over again as the pain suddenly returns.

"Breathe through it," Dash says, trying to comfort me.

"It's subsiding." I blow out a breath, knowing sweat now dots my made-up face.

Dash clears his throat. "We have time before the next contraction for me to get her out of here. In the meantime, you all go keep the family busy. Hopefully nobody will notice we're gone."

"Except Sasha and Xander, who we're sitting beside."

Linc takes a step closer. "I'll handle them and make sure they stay here until the movie ends." He grasps my hand and leans forward to kiss my cheek. "Good luck."

"Have a safe delivery," Jordan says.

Dash holds me close as we stay to the perimeter of the room, avoiding stopping to talk, and rushes her out. We'd taken a limo here, and Dash texts the driver. "I told him it's an emergency. He'll be outside any second."

We make it outside, find the driver, and I experience another contraction before Dash helps me into the back, where I lay across the seat, Dash squishing in and holding me.

"We're having a baby," he says, awe in his tone.

"If you're just figuring that out, we're in more trouble than I thought." I squeeze his hand tight and don't let go until we make it to the hospital.

★　★　★

Dash

I HOLD MY newborn baby against my bare chest, as I sit in a chair in Cassidy's hospital room, watching her sleep. Her bed is propped up, and she dozes, her head to one side. A guard stands outside, protecting my family from anyone who isn't welcome. I look down at the tiny infant, so pale and fragile against my darker skin and tattooed arms, and my heart feels full to bursting.

I wouldn't bring this up to anyone, but I whisper a silent prayer of thanks that my firstborn son is with the woman I love more than life itself and not some random groupie I'd hooked up with during my young and stupid days. I add into my gratitude the fact that Cassidy managed to have faith in me at a time I'd barely had any in myself.

"Hey," she says softly from the bed.

"Hey, yourself. How are you feeling? Need anything?" I ask. Being in the delivery room, watching what she went through, seeing my baby being born … I damned near passed out. I don't know how Cass hadn't. The doctor told us first babies usually take a long time, but not my son. Her contractions came faster, too fast for an epidural, and she was only in labor for four hours before our son was born.

"I'm okay. Can I have the baby who doesn't have a name?" A sweet smile curls her lips.

I rise, keeping the infant tight against me. I walk over and gently lay him on her chest. He didn't stir.

"How do you think the premiere went?" she asks, mentioning it for the first time.

"Linc texted earlier. He said the movie was a hit and got a standing ovation," I say, proud of my wife.

"That was probably because half the theater was family."

I roll my eyes. "Cute. Give yourself credit where it's due."

"Hey, what do you think was going on with Aurora? Is she okay?"

I frown. "Linc mentioned in text she wasn't feeling well and left early, which is not like her when it comes to family events."

Cassidy sighs. "Something about that Dare man triggered her. I wonder what it was?"

I shrug. "Guess we'll have to wait to find out. Linc

also mentioned he'd had to physically bar the doors to make sure the family stayed for the film. Sasha included."

Cassidy opens her mouth to speak when a nurse knocks and walks into the room. "You have a room full of people who want to take turns coming in. Two at a time, okay?"

"Are you up to visitors?" I ask Cassidy.

Tipping her head to the side, she says, "Do you really think I'd try and keep your mother out?"

I laugh then nod. "Tell them I'll be out in a few and bring them in two by two. Let them argue over who's first."

The nurse laughs and walks out.

"How about we name him before we have company because I had an idea?" she asks. We've been going around and around without coming up with anything before now.

I raise my brows. "Go for it."

"Well, given your rock star status, he needs a strong rock name. Axel is taken, like if Axl Rose spelled it differently…" She grins at her sort of joke. "But I was thinking about Freddie. He was *the* rock god, after all."

I'm shocked that she'd pick my idol's name. Even I hadn't offered it up because I was sure she'd turn it down. "You're sure?"

"Frederick … Freddie Kingston? I'm sure," she says, then yawns, rubbing the baby's back.

Peace, contentment, and love settles over me. "Freddie it is."

She smiles. "I love you, Dash, and I love our new little family." She holds up the infant and smiles. "I think he looks like me."

I let out a laugh. "Better you than me."

"I don't think so. After all, you're the sexy rock star in the family."

I lean over and press my lips to her forehead. "I love you, Cass, and don't you ever forget it."

"Back at you, Dash. You two," she says, looking down at the baby, "are my everything."

I wait a few minutes, allowing the emotions of the day to flow through me. Then I head out to deal with the family, the other people we love.

Thanks for reading! What's next?

Revisit Dash and Cassidy in a steamy short story,
JUST ANOTHER SPARK!

Then, Aurora Kingston is up next and her hero is a ….
Dare!

Continue The Kingston Family series as it transitions
to The Dirty Dares series with JUST ONE DARE!

Want even more Carly books?

CARLY'S BOOKLIST by Series – visit:
https://www.carlyphillips.com/CPBooklist

Sign up for Carly's Newsletter:
https://www.carlyphillips.com/CPNewsletter

Join Carly's Corner on Facebook:
https://www.carlyphillips.com/CarlysCorner

Carly on Facebook:
https://www.carlyphillips.com/CPFanpage

Carly on Instagram:
https://www.carlyphillips.com/CPInstagram

Carly's Booklist

newest series listed first

The Sterling Family

Book 1: Just One More Moment (Remington Sterling & Raven Walsh)

Book 2: Just One More Dare (Dex Kingston & Samantha Dare)

Book 3: Just One More Mistletoe (Max Corbin & Brandy Bloom)

Book 4: Just One More Temptation (Fallon Sterling & Noah Powers)

Book 5: Just One More Affair (Jared Sterling & Charlotte Kendall)

Book 6: Just One More Time (Aiden Sterling & Brooke Snyder)

Book 7: Just One More Date (Leo Watson & Camille Hendricks)

The Dirty Dares

Book 1: Just One Dare (Aurora Kingston & Nick Dare)

Book 2: Just One Kiss (Jade Dare & Knox Sinclair)

Book 3: Just One Taste (Asher Dare &

Nicolette Bettencourt)
Book 4: Just One Fling (Harrison Dare &
Winter Capwell)
Book 5: Just One Tease (Zach Dare &
Hadley Stevens)
Novella: Just One Summer (Maddox James &
Gabriella Davenport)

The Kingston Family
Book 1: Just One Night (Linc Kingston &
Jordan Greene)
Book 2: Just One Scandal (Chloe Kingston &
Beck Daniels)
Book 3: Just One Chance (Xander Kingston &
Sasha Keaton)
Book 4: Just One Spark (Dash Kingston &
Cassidy Forrester)
Just Another Spark – Short Story (Dash &
Cassidy revisited)
Novella: Just One Wish (Axel Forrester &
Tara Stillman)

Dare Nation
Book 1: Dare to Resist (Austin Prescott &
Quinn Stone)
Book 2: Dare to Tempt (Damon Prescott &
Evie Wolfe)
Book 3: Dare to Play (Jaxon Prescott & Macy Walker)

Book 4: Dare to Stay (Brandon Prescott &
Willow James)
Novella: Dare to Tease (Hudson Northfield &
Brianne Prescott)

** Paul Dare's sperm donor kids*

The Sexy Series
Book 1: More Than Sexy (Jason Dare &
Faith Lancaster)
Book 2: Twice As Sexy (Tanner Grayson &
Scarlett Davis)
Book 3: Better Than Sexy (Landon Bennett &
Vivienne Clark)
Novella: Sexy Love (Shane Warden & Amber Davis)

The Knight Brothers
Book 1: Take Me Again (Sebastian Knight &
Ashley Easton)
Novella: Take The Bride (Sierra Knight &
Ryder Hammond)
Book 2: Take Me Down (Parker Knight &
Emily Stevens)
Book 3: Dare Me Tonight (Ethan Knight &
Sienna Dare)
Take Me Now – Short Story (Harper Stevens &
Matt Banks)

The New York Dares

Book 1: Dare to Surrender (Gabe Dare & Isabelle Masters)

Book 2: Dare to Submit (Decklan Dare & Amanda Collins)

Book 3: Dare to Seduce (Max Savage & Lucy Dare)

Dare to Love Series

Book 1: Dare to Love (Ian Dare & Riley Taylor)

Book 2: Dare to Desire (Alex Dare & Madison Evans)

Book 3: Dare to Touch (Dylan Rhodes & Olivia Dare)

Book 4: Dare to Hold (Scott Dare & Meg Thompson)

Book 5: Dare to Rock (Avery Dare & Grey Kingston)

Book 6: Dare to Take (Tyler Dare & Ella Shaw)

A Very Dare Christmas – Short Story (Ian & Riley revisited)

** Sienna Dare gets together with Ethan Knight in **The Knight Brothers** (Dare Me Tonight).*

** Jason Dare gets together with Faith in the **Sexy Series** (More Than Sexy).*

** Kaden Barnes (you met him at the end of Dare to Take) has his own book in **The Billionaire Bad Boys** (Going Down Easy).*

For the most recent Carly books, visit CARLY'S BOOKLIST page

www.carlyphillips.com/CPBooklist

Other Indie Series

Billionaire Bad Boys
Book 1: Going Down Easy (Kaden Barnes & Lexie Parker)
Book 2: Going Down Fast (Lucas Monroe & Maxie Sullivan)
Book 3: Going Down Hard (Derek West & Cassie Storms)
Book 4: Going In Deep (Julian Dane & Kendall Parker)
Going Down Again – Short Story (Kade & Lexie revisited)

Bodyguard Bad Boys
Book 1: Rock Me (Ben Hollander & Summer Michelle)
Book 2: Tempt Me (Austin Rhodes & Mia Atwood)
Novella: His To Protect (Talia Shaw & Shane Landon)

Serendipity Series
Book 1: Serendipity (Ethan Barron & Faith Harrington)
Book 2: Kismet (Lissa Gardelli & Trevor Dane)
Book 3: Destiny (Nash Barron & Kelly Moss)
Book 4: Fated (Kate Andrews & Nick Mancini)
Book 5: Karma (Dare Barron & Liza McKnight)

Serendipity's Finest

Book 1: Perfect Fit (Michael Marsden & Cara Hartley)

Book 2: Perfect Fling (Erin Marsden & Cole Sanders)

Book 3: Perfect Together (Sam Marsden & Nicole Farnsworth)

Book 4: Perfect Strangers (Alexa Collins & Luke Thompson)

Hot Heroes Series

Book 1: Touch You Now (Halley Ward & Kane Harmon)

Book 2: Hold You Now (Phoebe Ward & Jake Nichols)

Book 3: Need You Now (Juliette Collins & Braden Clark)

Book 4: Want You Now (Andi Harmon & Kyle Davenport)

The Chandler Brothers

Book 1: The Bachelor (Roman Chandler & Charlotte Bronson)

Book 2: The Playboy (Rick Chandler & Kendall Sutton)

Book 3: The Heartbreaker (Chase Chandler & Sloane Carlisle)

The Lucky Series

Book 1: Lucky Charm (Derek Corwin &

Gabrielle Donovan)

Book 2: Lucky Streak (Mike Corwin& Amber
Rose Brennan)

Book 3: Lucky Break (Jason Corwin &
Lauren Perkins)

Costas Sisters

Book 1: Under the Boardwalk (Ariana Costas &
Quinn Donovan)

Book 2: Summer of Love (Zoe Costas &
Ryan Baldwin)

Ty and Hunter

Book 1: Cross My Heart (Lilly Dumont & Ty Benson)

Book 2: Sealed with a Kiss (Molly Gifford &
Daniel Hunter)

The Hot Zone

Book 1: Hot Stuff (Annabelle Jordan &
Brandon Vaughn)

Book 2: Hot Number (Micki Jordan & Damian Fuller)

Book 3: Hot Item (Sophie Jordan & Riley Nash)

Book 4: Hot Property (Amy Stone & John Roper)

The Simply Series

Book 1: Simply Sinful (Kayla Luck &
Kane McDermott)

Book 2: Simply Scandalous (Catherine Luck &

Logan Montgomery)
Book 3: Simply Sensual (Ben Callahan &
Grace Montgomery)
Book 4: Body Heat (Jake Lowell & Brianne Nelson)
Book 5: Simply Sexy (Rina Lowell & Colin Lyons)

The Most Eligible Bachelor Series
Book 1: Kiss Me if You Can (Sam Cooper &
Lexie Davis)
Book 2: Love Me If You Dare (Rafe Mancuso &
Sara Rios)

Carly Classics
Book 1: The Right Choice (Carly Wexler &
Mike Novak)
Book 2: Perfect Partners (Chelsie Russell &
Griffin Stuart)
Book 3: Unexpected Chances (Dylan North &
Holly Evans)
Book 4: Worthy of Love (Kevin Manning &
Nikki Welles)

For the most recent Carly books, visit CARLY'S
BOOKLIST page
www.carlyphillips.com/CPBooklist

Stand-Alone Books

The Seduction – Kindle Worlds, The Arrangement Universe – No Longer Available

More Than Words Volume 7 – Compassion

Can't Wait

Naughty Under the Mistletoe

Grey's Anatomy 101 Essay

For the most recent Carly books, visit CARLY'S BOOKLIST page

www.carlyphillips.com/CPBooklist

About the Author

NY Times, Wall Street Journal, and USA Today Bestseller, Carly Phillips is the queen of Alpha Heroes, at least according to The Harlequin Junkie Reviewer. Carly married her college sweetheart and lives in Purchase, NY along with her crazy dogs who are featured on her Facebook and Instagram pages. The author of over 75 romance novels, she has raised two incredible daughters and is now an empty nester. Carly's book, The Bachelor, was chosen by Kelly Ripa as her first romance club pick. Carly loves social media and interacting with her readers. Want to keep up with Carly? Sign up for her newsletter and receive TWO FREE books at www.carlyphillips.com.

www.ingramcontent.com/pod-product-compliance
Lightning Source LLC
Chambersburg PA
CBHW071234190726
48292CB00007B/2275